TO HEAL A BROKEN EARL

The Rakes of Mayhem
Book 7

Anna St. Claire

ARE YOU SIGNED UP FOR DRAGONBLADE'S BLOG?

You'll get the latest news and information on exclusive giveaways, exclusive excerpts, coming releases, sales, free books, cover reveals and more.

Check out our complete list of authors, too!

No spam, no junk. That's a promise!

Sign Up Here

www.dragonbladepublishing.com

Dearest Reader;

Thank you for your support of a small press. At Dragonblade Publishing, we strive to bring you the highest quality Historical Romance from some of the best authors in the business. Without your support, there is no 'us', so we sincerely hope you adore these stories and find some new favorite authors along the way.

Happy Reading!

CEO, Dragonblade Publishing

Additional Dragonblade books by Author Anna St. Claire

The Rakes of Mayhem Series
The Earl of Excess (Book 1)
The Marquess of Mischief (Book 2)
The Duke of Disorder (Book 3)
The Baron's Return (Book 4)
To Win a Viscount's Heart (Book 5)
Tempting a Lonely Lord (Book 6)
To Heal a Broken Earl (Book 7)
A Gift for Agatha (Novella)

The Lyon's Den Series
Lyon's Prey
The Heart of a Lyon
Once Upon a Winter's Tale (Novella)
A Lyon of Her Own

Also from Anna St. Claire
Once upon a Haunted Heart (Novella)

CHAPTER ONE

No. 3 Market Street
Shepherd Market, Mayfair, London
Spring 1819

W*HAT A BEAUTIFUL day,* Emma thought as she walked along the shoreline of Brighton Beach. *What could be the harm in going barefoot in the water?* Glancing over her shoulder, she saw she was alone. Smiling with anticipation, Emma removed her halfboots and stockings and waded into the surf, not caring that the bottom of her dress was soaked and clinging to her legs. She loved the ocean—loved walking through the crest of each wave as it lapped against the shore.

There was a contentment here that she'd only ever found by the sea. She reveled in the soothing coolness of the water, the soft squish of the sand between her toes, the steady roar of the breaking waves, and the clean, salt-sweet scent of the sea spray. Emma loved everything about the shore. Closing her eyes, she tilted her face to the sun, smiling at the warming glow. The sun felt more than warm. Quite hot, really.

"Ow!" she mumbled. Something—or rather someone—had just tugged on her braid. "Stop that! Ow!"

Another tug.

"Stop pulling on my braid," she muttered again, this time more loudly.

"Auntie Emma! Auntie Emma!"

Emma's eyes flew open. Her four-year-old niece, Katherine, stood beside the bed, her small fingers tangled in Emma's braid, her lip trembling.

"Katie, what's the matter?" Emma asked. Katie's dark auburn curls mirrored her father's, as did her eyes—now wide and worried—a warm brown instead of the striking violet eyes that Emma and Evie shared as sisters.

"There's someone outside," Katie whispered, glancing toward the window. "He was looking up at us. At first, I thought he was a nice man because he did something that Papa always does."

"And what's that?" Emma asked, still thinking Katie had had one of her nightmares. Katie was prone to bad dreams and often woke during the night. Emma frequently brought Katie to the small carriage house her sister and brother-in-law had built for her. This arrangement allowed Evie—who was pregnant with her second child—to get some sleep. It had become routine since Emma moved in several months ago.

"This." Katie held her index finger over her lips and furrowed her brow, indicating she should be quiet.

"So, if he did something your Papa does, then why is he bad?"

"Because Papa always smiles and laughs. The man at the window wasn't smiling. Not at all. His eyes looked mean and scary."

"Well, we can't have that," Emma said. If she didn't look out the window, Katie wouldn't be able to go back to sleep.

Evie and her husband, Martin, had traveled to Martin's parents' home in Essex for a funeral. His elderly Aunt Sarah had recently passed away. Emma had only met the woman once—at the wedding—but remembered her as a gentle soul. Evie had been as distraught as Martin over his aunt's death.

"Aunt Sarah was the first person to truly welcome me into the family," her sister had wept. "She was almost like another mother to me."

Evie had asked Emma to look after Katie while she and Martin were away. Emma was honored that her sister and brother-in-law trusted her with their daughter. They were her closest family—her only family—and Emma would do anything for her niece.

"I fear she will get into mischief at Martin's family estate," Evie had confessed. "His brother and wife will be there, but their girls are probably staying home with their governess. His mother has always claimed to have a delicate constitution, and you know how she gets when there are children and animals around. We brought Katie to visit when she was two, and she accidentally knocked over a vase and chipped it. Martin's mother practically fainted. So, we think it's best if we don't bring her with us. It works better to visit his parents when they come to London for the Season."

Evie had not exaggerated her concerns.

Martin's mother and father were nothing like him. Martin's first instinct was always to make guests feel welcome and comfortable in his home. His parents, however, were rigid, prudish, and unyielding. Visitors were expected to abide by their rules without exception, and they rarely made concessions for anyone, not even their children.

Aunt Sarah had been the exception. She had welcomed Evie with open arms.

In his youth, Martin and his siblings—an older brother and younger sister—had spent weeks at Aunt Sarah's home while their parents were in London for the Season, and Aunt Sarah had had a tremendous influence on him. Her home had been filled with laughter, affection, and sweet memories—everything childhood ought to be.

Emma pushed back the quilts and rose from the warm co-coon of her bed, slid on her slippers, and padded to the window.

She loved her bedroom. She loved everything about her quaint quarters and was grateful to her sister and brother-in-law for everything they had done for her.

"You need your comfort and privacy, Emma," Martin had insisted.

He had added a cozy parlor on the first floor, complete with a floor-to-ceiling, wall-to-wall bookcase for her extensive collection, and a seating area where she could entertain friends and invite people for tea.

Incredibly generous and thoughtful, Martin had also built a bathing chamber at the back, complete with her very own cistern and hearth to heat water, similar to the one he had built for himself and Evie in their rooms. Upstairs, he had crafted a bright, airy bedroom just for her.

Emma had been overwhelmed by their kindness, thankful to have such a loving sister and brother-in-law who cared enough to make her feel truly welcome while also giving her the privacy and independence she valued.

Looking out the window, Emma gasped. She was shocked to see smoke billowing from the back of her sister's home. Perhaps the fire was confined to the kitchen. Maybe she could put it out. But she couldn't leave Katie alone.

"Did you see him, Auntie?" Katie asked, her voice small.

"No, sweetie," Emma said quickly, running back to her. "Where are your shoes, Katie?"

"What's wrong, Auntie Emma? Why do I need to wear my shoes?"

"Because there's a fire in the house, sweetie, and we have to get to safety."

Grabbing Katie's shoes from beside the washstand, Emma slipped them on the child's feet, her fingers surprisingly steady. She pulled Katie's robe on her, then her own, moving swiftly.

Snatching two washcloths from the washstand, she wet them in the water basin and tucked them into her pocket. Taking Katie's hand firmly in hers, Emma led her down the stairs, out the carriage house door, and toward the main house.

Unlocking the back door, Emma and Katie both coughed as a cloud of smoke poured out and surrounded them.

Taking one of the cloths from her pocket, Emma handed it to Katie. "Put this over your nose and stay close to me. Don't let go of my hand," she said.

"I won't, I promise," Katie said, placing the wet cloth over her face.

Emma hugged her close, tightening her arm around the small body beside her. She needed to question Katie more about the man, but right now, the fire came first. If it were confined to the kitchen, she might be able to put it out before it spread.

Yesterday, she had given the servants two days off. *What could possibly go wrong?* Now, every possibility ran through her mind like a stampede. What if someone had forgotten to dampen the hearth before leaving? What if the fire was already too far gone?

Shaking her head to clear her thoughts, Emma withdrew the second cloth and covered her nose. Tugging Katie firmly behind her, she rushed down the hallway that led to the kitchen. She flung open the door and stared in horror. *Everything* was on fire. Flames licked greedily up the walls, devouring everything in their path. There was nothing to be done. The fire was too far gone—it would soon claim the rest of the house.

She had to act swiftly.

Tightening her hold on Katie, Emma turned, guiding them down the hall toward Martin's study.

She rushed inside, pulling Katie with her, and slammed the door behind them. Martin had shown her where the household funds were when she first moved in—just in case she ever needed money.

Opening Martin's desk drawer, Emma felt around for the small bag of coins and bills. Her fingers brushed familiar velvet, and she grabbed it.

Glancing up, she saw smoke streaming in from beneath the door. Time was running out. Heart pounding, she stuffed the bag into the pocket of her robe. Grabbing Katie's hand, she felt the door. Relieved it wasn't hot, Emma opened it.

Smoke swirled into the room, thick and choking. Both Emma and Katie began coughing again. "Hold your cloth over your face, sweetie," Emma said as she scooped Katie up, turned the child's face against her shoulder, and hugged her close. Saying a small prayer, she made a mad dash down the hall, out the door, and back to the carriage house.

Running up the stairs, she set Katie down and grabbed her valise, stuffing it with as much clothing as she could manage.

Katie coughed again, and Emma grabbed a cup from her bedside table, filling it with water from the pitcher on her washstand.

"There's so much smoke, Auntie Emma," Katie said after draining the cup. "More smoke than when Daddy smokes his pipe."

"It's all right, sweetie. We're going on an adventure. But you must be brave and do exactly what I say. It's very important. Do I have your promise?" Emma asked.

"Yes, Auntie. Pinkie promise."

Katie held out her little finger, and Emma hooked hers around it, squeezing tight.

Putting on her pelisse and helping Katie into her coat, Emma guided her niece back downstairs and hurried to the stable. "Katie, we're going to ride to a safe place—away from the fire."

"Will we come back and get my toys?" Katie asked, her voice small and hopeful.

"Maybe, sweetie. Right now, we need to find help." Emma squeezed Kaite's hand and added in a whisper, "You remember Lady Beadle, don't you?"

"Yes. I remember her. She's the nice lady who always gives me lemon biscuits," Katie said, a tiny smile breaking through.

"That's right, sweetie," Emma said, forcing a cheerful note into her voice. "I'm sure Lady Beadle will have plenty of biscuits waiting for you."

Thank goodness she knew Lady Celia Armstrong and her aunt, Viscountess Millicent Beadle, Emma thought as they reached the stable.

She knew it was only a matter of time before the fire exploded into a full inferno, probably engulfing everything, including the stable and her beautiful carriage house. "Stay close while I saddle the horses, Katie," Emma said.

"What about Mama and Papa? They won't know how to find us," Katie whimpered, clutching her little doll tighter.

Emma hadn't even seen her pick up the doll—but Polly was almost always tucked under the child's arm.

"Polly wants Mama," Katie whispered.

Emma crouched down, tapping the tip of Katie's nose. "Polly needs to be a brave little dolly—just like you, poppet," she said gently. "I know you can reassure Polly that your mama and papa will find us. I promise." She gave Katie's hand a soft squeeze. "Can you do that for me? Can you help Polly be brave just like you?"

Katie nodded solemnly. "Yes, Auntie Emma." She hugged Polly close and whispered into the doll's ear, "Everything will be all right."

As Emma saddled the horses, questions swirled through her mind. *How did the fire start? Who is the strange man that Katie was talking about?* Then there were the tragic stories of a recent slew of fires that had plagued London.

Just last week, a townhouse went up in flames, killing an older couple inside. There had been no identifiable cause, except arson—and to her knowledge, no suspect, no motive. Emma had seen the burned-out shell of a house herself as she, Celia, and Lady Beadle drove past on the way to the orphanage, where they volunteered every week. The sight had been shocking and deeply disturbing.

Unwilling to succumb to the emotions and the tears that threatened to overwhelm her, Emma focused on her task. She quickly slipped the halters on the two horses housed in the stable. Even though she wouldn't need it tonight, she strapped her sister's favorite saddle onto her mare and saddled Martin's gelding for the ride ahead. Lady Beadle lived a short distance away. Once they arrived safely, Emma would send word to Celia and Martin. In her short time here, Lady Beadle and Celia had become dear friends—and Emma trusted that they would know what to do.

She lifted Katie onto Martin's horse and swung up behind her, steadying the child in front of her. Gripping the lead rope for her sister's mare, Emma urged the gelding into motion. Together, they headed to Curzon Street and safety.

But moments later, the hairs on the back of her neck prickled, and a shiver raced down her spine.

Someone was watching them.

But who? Where?

Glancing over her shoulder, she saw him.

A man stood in the shadow of a streetlamp, leaning against a tree, his hat pulled low over his brow. He wore a great black cape, the hem stirring slightly in the breeze.

It's him—she knew it.

The man Katie had seen at the window.

The man who had started the fire.

We need to get out of here. Now.

Dimly, she heard the distant shouts of men and women, the frantic ringing of alarm bells. Emma pulled Katie closer against her and urged the gelding to a faster pace, keeping a tight grip on the reins.

They had seen the arsonist.

Worse—he had seen *them*.

CHAPTER TWO

No. 14 Upper Brook Street
Near Grosvenor Square, Mayfair
London, England

"**D**AMN AND BLAST!"

The door to the bedroom flew open, and a tall, wiry blond man hurried inside. "My lord! I see you're...in a bit of a predicament."

"A predicament?" Michael snapped. "What gave you that impression, Hastings? The fact that I'm lying here on my naked arse in a puddle of ice-cold water?"

His tone was sharp enough to cut glass, given the situation was anything but dignified. He cast a glare toward the chair near the bed, where Hastings had left a towel neatly folded for him. If he'd had the sense—or the humility—to ask Hastings to move the chair closer before he climbed into the tub, he might not have slipped trying to reach it.

But pride, as always, had won out over caution.

"Quite right, my lord," Hastings said, his lips twitching. "Though, had you rung the bell"—he nodded pointedly toward the small table beside the tub—"I might have been able to prevent your current...situation."

"Help me up, will you?" Michael grumbled.

"Why didn't you ring for me?" Hastings pressed, moving forward but making no real effort to hide his amusement.

"Because I'm tired of ringing that damn bell like some cranky codger in his dotage, that's why," Michael muttered as Hastings helped him to his feet.

Hastings pursed his lips. "Well, you certainly aren't *old*, my lord."

Michael shot him a sideways glare. "Glad to hear it."

Hastings gave a bland shrug. "Cranky, perhaps. Stubborn, most assuredly. But not *old*."

"Stop, Hastings—your compliments are making me blush," Michael said dryly.

Hastings snorted—a familiar sound, one Michael had heard often enough on the battlefield and in far darker places than this room. Without another word, Hastings steadied him, guiding him toward the bed with the same quiet efficiency that had once saved Michael's life more times than he could count.

Michael clenched his teeth, lowering himself onto the mattress with a hiss. His left leg was throbbing mercilessly.

Hastings, wiping the floor, glanced at him and said with dry precision, "Perhaps next time you'll ask for assistance, my lord."

Michael exhaled slowly, his face tightening. "Like hell, I will," he muttered.

Hastings wisely said nothing at first. Then, with a twitch of his lips, he murmured, "Miracles do happen."

Michael pointedly ignored his valet's smart reply. He shifted his weight—and pain lanced through his thigh. His leg had never truly healed—not after the war, and certainly not after he'd been shot, stabbed, and left to drown in a brackish sea cave on the Isle of Wight.

He was lucky he still had it, though some days, it hardly felt like much of a victory.

Seeing him grimace, Hastings added, "You know, my lord, if you would only heed Dr. Enzo Bianchi's advice, you might not be in such pain. He is much sought after. Even Wellington himself recommends the Italian."

Michael grunted. "Yes, so you say."

"When was the last time you allowed me to massage the salve into your leg?" Hastings asked.

"When?" Michael growled, his voice rough with pain. "Surely you remember the last time. Finn woke from his sleep, started howling, and made a quick exit as if he were running for his life." He grimaced. "My dog ran away because I reeked, Hastings."

"Aye, I recall," Hastings said. "Finn hid until mealtime the next day, and that dog never runs from anything."

"Especially a meal." Michael rubbed a hand over his face, half in amusement, half in misery.

Finn never missed a meal.

Michael's mind flickered back to the scruffy, half-starved spaniel he'd found during a mission in France. A special assignment had sent him and his team undercover to hunt down a dangerous smuggler. While inspecting a ship moored off the coast of Brittany, he'd come across a small crate tucked into the hull, housing a trembling, malnourished dog. The crew claimed they'd found the spaniel wandering the woodlands, appearing half-dead.

It had taken months for Finn to trust him—and to get the dog healthy. He had been in the crate, forgotten, for too long, and the dog had little muscle tone. Now, the dog was his constant companion—unless the cursed salve came out. Then loyalty fled faster than French smugglers spotting a revenue cutter.

"Speaking of Finn, where is he? He's usually sleeping on his bed near the fireplace," Michael said, glancing toward the empty spot.

"When I came in earlier to lay out your clothing, Finn got the scent of something our Mrs. Peppers was baking for tomorrow morning, and took off for the kitchen," Hastings said. "Last I checked, she was baking scones and biscuits. I imagine Finn is huddled at her side, and we both know Mrs. McDonald can't resist those big brown eyes. No doubt he'll gobble up as much as she gives him. They've bonded over her cooking."

"Traitorous dog," Michael murmured fondly.

"There's no need for you to subject yourself to being in pain all the time. It's all about your pride, my lord," Hastings said. "The stuff works. At least allow me to massage it into your leg at night. No one will be around to smell it."

Hastings cared. He'd been with Michael for nearly ten years. Since serving as his batman during the war, he'd continued at his side, assisting him in his work for the Crown. They were more than lord and valet; they were friends. Michael didn't always like what Hastings said, but he listened.

"I understand, my lord," Hastings said as if reading his thoughts. "Had the second injury not happened on that special assignment, you might only be dealing with the limp."

"Yes, I know what you are going to say…*again*. Had I allowed you to accompany me on the assignment, this might not have happened. You keep reminding me," Michael ground out. "But as I've told you many times, that wasn't an option."

"No. I was going to add that Dr. Bianchi's salve is a tried-and-true remedy. When you used it those first few times, it gave you relief. And as you are aware, you might have lost your leg—nay, your life—had your good friends not taken you to Lord and Lady Romney's residence. And I don't have to remind you that Lady Romney—who grew up in America's Louisiana bayou country and learned herbal medicine from her aunts—saved your life with her expertise."

"Your point?" Michael huffed.

"My point, my lord, is that you are fortunate, and owe much of that good fortune to these herbal remedies. Yes, it smells abominable, and no, we've no idea what's actually in the concoction—but it does work."

"Fine. I'll allow it," Michael reluctantly agreed. Since returning to England, he had become more isolated. His life had changed. He kept to himself more, unaffected by the winsome smiles of young ladies who tried to capture his attention at social gatherings. He reclined back, adjusted the towel over his frame, and extended his leg for Hastings's ministrations.

Afterward, as he lay there with a scented handkerchief over his nose, doing everything he could not to breathe in the pungent odor, the door burst open, and his butler swooped in.

"Damn and blast! Doesn't anyone knock anymore?" Michael said, trying to sit up, while at the same time keeping the smelly salve from staining his coverlet and holding the handkerchief over his nose.

"My lord…forgive the intrusion, but we have a situation," the butler said, breathing hard.

"Stanhope, this better be good," Michael said, tossing the useless handkerchief aside. He could still smell the salve anyway.

Stanhope took one sniff and immediately pinched his nose. Michael bit back a chuckle at the hilarious look on the older man's face. Stanhope could barely tolerate any strong aromas; even a lady's perfume brought a pinched look to his face that made him resemble a cat that had just tasted soured milk. The foul smell of the salve might give him a fit of the vapors.

"My lord, forgive me, but there's an emergency at Lady Beadle's. There's been a fire, and Lady Beadle needs you right away."

My God! She's like an aunt to me. I must get there as soon as possible.

"Have my horse brought to the front, Stanhope," Michael said.

"Yes, my lord," the butler said, his eyes watering and his finger still pressed beneath his nose as he hastily left the bedchamber.

A moment later, a footman entered, leading Finn on a leash—just as Michael stood and tossed the towel on the bed, exposing himself to man and beast. Michael heaved a beleaguered sigh. His bedchamber was beginning to resemble a public house.

The footman's eyes widened, and his cheeks flushed scarlet. Turning his gaze away, he cleared his throat. "My lord, Mrs. Peppers said to tell you that Master Finn has had his fill of sausage rolls, scones, and biscuits, and asked that I escort him to your rooms."

Snatching the towel back off the bed, Michael wrapped it around his lower torso. "Thank you, Thomas," he muttered.

Finn made a strange noise as he sniffed the air. With a sudden yelp, he jerked the leash from the footman's hand and bolted from the room. The footman exclaimed and chased after him.

CHAPTER THREE

No. 25 Curzon Street
Near Shepherd's Square, Mayfair
London, England

THE WHOLE NIGHT felt like a scene from one of the Gothic novels Emma loved to read. But there was nothing to love about her sister's home burning to the ground at the hands of an evil arsonist. She closed her eyes and counted to ten before opening them, praying that when she did, she would find herself back in her room, with Katie tucked safely next to her, and a storybook in her hands. But when she opened her eyes, she was still in the drawing room at Lady Beadle's, with Katie perched on her lap, giggling as she watched the dowager's cats bat paws at each other and meow.

Had it been three hours since they'd left their home and arrived at Lady Beadle's doorstep? It felt like a lifetime.

Emma and Katie arrived, soot-streaked and exhausted, in the mid-dle of the night.

Within moments, the butler kindly opened the door, his face show-ing immediate concern as he took in their bedraggled state.

"Lady Grantham, how can I assist you?" he asked, holding a candle aloft to light the darkened hall.

"I'm s-so sorry to wake you at this hour, Jenkins. But we need help," Emma said, between wheezing and coughing. She was still feeling the effects of the smoke she and Katie had inhaled. Thankfully, Katie's

coughing had eased during the ride to Lady Beadle's.

Jenkins quickly ushered them into the vestibule.

"Could we possibly see Lady Beadle? Our…h-house…b-burned down, and Katie and I have no p-place to go."

"My dear lady… I am so deeply sorry," the butler said, his voice and face reflecting shock.

"Thank you, Jenkins," she said, hugging Katie closer to her side. "There was a strange man… I think he set the fire." Her voice sounded strained and hoarse to her ears.

"Good God!" the older man said, horror tightening his features. He immediately turned to one of the footmen standing behind him. "Wake the stable hands and see that the horses are settled."

"Yes, sir," the young man said, hurrying away.

Emma's nerves had begun to fray, as they often did once the worst of a crisis had passed—that delayed, trembling fear.

"I…I wondered if I could get word to Lady Armstrong," she said, her voice uneven.

Emma had never been a fragile, wilting flower, unlike many of the debutantes in Society who fluttered their fans and simpered behind them. But tonight, with her sister and brother-in-law away and no familiar comfort nearby, she had needed the steady, reassuring presence of her friend.

Without hesitation, Jenkins turned to the remaining footman.

"Go at once and fetch Lord and Lady Armstrong," he instructed the man, his voice low and urgent. "Make haste."

The other young man nodded and rushed off just as a tapping sound echoed behind them.

"My dear Emma," Lady Beadle said, approaching them, her cane thumping briskly against the polished marble floor as she walked.

Jenkins turned and bowed slightly. "My lady, forgive the commotion, but Lady Grantham and her niece have been through a terrible ordeal."

"I can see that," Lady Beadle said, her voice softening. She reached out and enveloped Emma and Katie in a warm hug. "My dears, let us help you."

Emma blinked back tears and murmured her thanks, overwhelmed by the dowager's kindness.

"Come, let us sit in the drawing room," Lady Beadle said briskly,

patting Emma's arm. "I'm sure Celia and William will be here soon. Yes, Jenkins, I heard you tell Reggie to fetch them," she added with a faint smile as the butler opened his mouth once more to explain. "The drawing room will be better suited. It's larger, and I fear there will be a full house before we get this all sorted."

She turned to Jenkins once more. "Now, be a dear and bring us some good, strong tea, warm milk for Katie, and a plate of those delicious lemon biscuits Mrs. Peppers made earlier. Oh, and prepare a guest chamber for Emma and Katie. The blue room—it's so soothing. I am certain they will want to rest and revive themselves after their ordeal. And bring us clean cloths and a bowl of warm water for washing."

"Yes, my lady," Jenkins said promptly, and he escorted them to the drawing room and saw to their comfort.

Emma sighed with relief as Lady Beadle took charge. She was too exhausted to think clearly.

Once they had been settled, Lady Beadle tapped her cane lightly against the floor. "Jenkins, could you retrieve my hearing horn? I need to hear everything Lady Grantham tells me, so I don't miss any important details."

"Yes, mistress," the butler said in a bland voice. He crossed to a small cabinet beside the door, withdrew a conical black-and-brass hearing device, and handed it to the dowager with practiced efficiency.

"Ah! Now, then. This will do the trick," Lady Beadle said, adjusting the horn to her ear.

Emma knew that Lady Beadle was hard of hearing. Celia had told her, with a chuckle, that her aunt could read lips perfectly well—but she preferred the ear horn for dramatic effect. She enjoyed seeing the long-suffering look on Jenkins's face every time she asked him to retrieve it—and she loved to complain about the blasted thing.

Seeing the butler still standing beside them, Lady Beadle asked, "Was there something else, Jenkins?"

"Yes, my lady. With your permission, I will instruct several of our footmen to check the perimeter of the house to ensure Lady Grantham and her young niece were not followed."

Lady Beadle nodded. "Sound judgment, Jenkins. As usual, you are several steps ahead of me," the older woman said, smiling in his direction.

"Meow…"

"Lady Beadle, your kittens are so funny. They make me laugh," Katie said, giggling, bringing Emma out of her reverie.

"Yes, they are rather cheeky pusses, aren't they, my dear?" Lady Beadle said, smiling as she dangled a long feather on a stick before them.

Emma regarded her hostess, wishing she, too, could laugh at the precocious cats chasing the feather. She had done her best to remain calm while she relayed the events of the night to Lady Beadle, but now, as they waited for Celia and Armstrong to arrive, she could feel her emotions bubbling up again, like a tidal wave.

"My dear Emma, may I offer you another cup of tea?" Lady Beadle asked in a kind voice. "I find tea to be most restorative after a shock."

"No, thank you, my lady," Emma said, hearing the tremor in her voice.

"You have endured a horrendous ordeal," the old woman said gently, "but I promise you—even after the darkest night, the sun will always rise."

Emma nodded, sniffling back tears. "I know, Lady Beadle… But the fire… Everything is gone." She swallowed hard as if something large and painful were lodged in her throat, so swollen it was. Her sister's beautiful home…the lovely carriage house… Both had likely been completely destroyed.

"You're safe, my dear, and that is what counts," Lady Beadle said softly as if reading her thoughts. "Houses can be rebuilt. New gowns can be sewn. But a life, once lost, is lost forever."

Emma took a deep breath and let it out slowly.

Lady Beadle was right.

They were alive.

They were safe from the fire.

Safe from *him*.

Emma had no idea who the man was, nor why he had set the fire. But she knew without a doubt that it had been him, standing so nonchalantly beneath the lamppost, as though he were watching a cricket match instead of a house burning to the ground.

But why?

"I fear I may have brought terrible trouble to your door," Emma said, her voice cracking. Despite her attempts to stop them, tears began to stream down her face. "Only I didn't know where else to turn."

"Of course, you did the right thing coming here," Lady Beadle said in a reassuring tone. "And I have lived through and overcome plenty of troubling times, my dear—and so will you." She smiled as she reached for a navy velvet cord and tugged it.

Jenkins appeared a few moments later.

"My lady, how may I be of service?"

"Jenkins, please ask Doris to join us," Lady Beadle said, gesturing to Katie, who had fallen asleep.

Emma shifted the child on her lap, tucking Katie's head onto her shoulder.

"Right away, my lady," the older man said. He bobbed a quick nod and left.

"Emma, you must stay with us as long as you need," Lady Beadle said. "We will do everything in our power to put things to rights."

Before Emma could answer, a sweet-faced older woman rushed into the drawing room.

"Ah, there you are, Doris," Lady Beadle said.

"My lady, the blue room has been prepared for your guests."

"Excellent, Doris. You remember Lady Grantham. She and her niece have escaped a horrible fire at Mr. Martin Saunders's home. Mr. Saunders is my solicitor, and he and his wife Evie are dear friends, as you know."

Katie stirred on Emma's lap. "Auntie Emma, did you see the man?" she murmured in a sleepy voice. The little girl sat up, wiped the sleep from her eyes, and looked around. "Can they help us, Auntie?"

"Of course we will, little lamb," Lady Beadle interjected, nonplussed by Katie's question. "And you must both call me Millie."

Katie shook her head. "Mama told me always to ask and not *as-thume*," she said.

"Your mama is a wise woman," Lady Beadle said with a smile. "I would love to have two more nieces. How about you call me *Auntie* Millie?"

Katie gave a sleepy nod.

"Now then, we have a pretty bedchamber all ready for you. Doris can take you upstairs and help you get settled."

"But what about Auntie Emma?"

"I'll be fine here," Emma said, kissing Katie on the forehead.

"But Polly gets scared at night," Katie said, hugging her cloth doll close to her chest.

"Doris will stay with you and Polly the entire time," Lady Beadle said.

"Yes, indeed," Doris said, her voice soft and gentle. "Do you like bedtime stories?"

Katie nodded, her face lighting up. "Polly likes bedtime stories too."

"I'm ever so glad to hear that. Because I love reading bedtime stories." The older maid smiled. "How about we get you a warm glass of milk with some honey, and then I'll read you and Polly a story. Does that sound acceptable?"

"That sounds really good." Katie beamed. "As long as Auntie Emma comes later."

"I will, sweetheart. I promise," Emma said, hugging Katie tight.

Doris took Katie's hand, but before they left, Katie turned and ran to Lady Beadle, hugging her and kissing her on the cheek.

"Thank you, Auntie Millie. For everything."

"Oh, you are most welcome, my sweet child," the older woman said, blinking back tears.

A SHORT WHILE later, Celia swept into the drawing room, her vibrant green gown fluttering around her as she rushed to Emma's side and wrapped her arms around her. Some of Emma's restlessness dissipated in the warmth of her friend's hug.

Jenkins followed behind, along with Celia's husband, Lord William Armstrong. Dressed impeccably in a tailored charcoal-gray suit that accentuated his dignified presence, Armstrong moved with the quiet confidence of a man accustomed to taking charge.

"You, poor dear—we cannot imagine what you've been through," Celia said. "Where is Katie?"

"Doris took her upstairs. The wee child was exhausted," Lady Beadle interjected.

Armstrong cleared his throat. "Lady Grantham…Emma, we are thankful that you and Katie are safe. You were very brave and resourceful. Can you tell us what you saw?"

Emma nodded. "Katie woke me up and told me she saw a man outside. I looked out the window of the carriage house to see if there was anyone in the yard and instead saw smoke billowing from the house." She drew in a shaky breath. "Thinking it may have been a candle left alight—or perhaps the hearth in the kitchen had not been properly banked—we dressed and rushed into the house, only to discover the entire kitchen was up in flames." Emma pressed a hand briefly against her chest.

"There was nothing we could do other than escape. I packed what little we could and saddled the horses. As we were leaving, I saw a man across the street…standing there. Just watching. I believe it was the arsonist." Her voice faltered for a moment. "I didn't get a good look at him—he was standing in the shadows. But Katie had seen him earlier from the window. What's worse— he saw us. He knows we can identify him." Her gaze swept over Armstrong, Celia, and Lady Beadle. "We must get word to Evie and Martin. They're in Essex at the funeral of Martin's late aunt."

"I have a concern—one that I feel could be important, and I think I have an idea on how to fix that concern," Lady Beadle said. "Emma fears that she brought trouble here. I'm not worried about that, but I do believe if you and your niece saw the arsonist, he may be looking for you. A good friend of our family, Lord Michael Wilton, is a former agent of the Crown and fought against Old Boney. He lives a quiet life primarily at his country estate and has mentioned he plans to hire a housekeeper at the Sussex residence. I think it would be the perfect place for you and Katie to stay while Armstrong and his friends track down this cursed villain."

"Oh, but I couldn't possibly impose on Lord Wilton's privacy." Emma did not feel comfortable accepting charity.

"You're already acquainted with Michael's sister, Lizzy, who is married to my brother, Baron Edward Sinclair," Celia added, patting Emma's hand.

"I do remember them. They are a lovely couple," Emma said. She had met Lizzy and Sinclair at a dinner at Celia and Armstrong's townhouse last month. The recently married couple were both kind and charming. "But that does not change the fact that I do not wish to be a burden."

Emma and Evie had lost both parents at an early age and lived with various relatives over the years until Evie married Martin and sent for Emma once they had established a proper home. Although they had been educated as genteel young women, they had never truly felt as though they belonged.

Emma needed to find some sort of living arrangement for her and Katie. She had spent her formative years among the household staff, learning a great deal from kindly cooks and housekeepers, butlers and maids, and even stable masters and grooms. She'd confided as much to Lady Beadle, who had completely understood.

"I admire your independent spirit, my dear," Lady Beadle said with a wink. "And I may have a suggestion that could resolve this entire situation. Lord Wilton has recently inherited his earldom and discovered that all his estates have been sadly neglected for years—all except his London townhouse. He is looking for a housekeeper for his country estate in Sussex. It's a small manor house and needs some renovations, but it is not in as poor condition as his main estate in Preston or his third estate in Lancashire. Most importantly, he prefers Sussex and intends to renovate it to make it his home. I believe this could be a perfect place for you and little Katie. You would not only be safe, but you would also be assisting Lord Wilton. It is an ideal solution!"

"I would be delighted to work as a housekeeper, Lady Beadle," Emma said.

"The position with Lord Wilton—Michael—would be for a short time," Celia said, turning to her husband. "Just until we get everything sorted, isn't that right, dear?"

"Yes, of course," Armstrong replied. "I think the idea has merit. We'll get word to Martin and Evie to remain where they are and suggest they hire more men to guard his family's estate as a precautionary measure."

Emma felt a wave of relief. Armstrong would be able to get word to Martin swiftly, and she would be able to keep Katie safe without feeling like a burden.

"While you and Katie are safely ensconced at Wilton's estate, we'll be searching for this vile brute," Armstrong continued. "I am almost positive the arsonist who set fire to your home is the same one connected with similar fires around London for the past several months. We need to find this devil and bring him to justice."

"Michael recently arrived in London on business," Lady Beadle said. "I'm certain he is still here."

"Indeed, Michael's eager to escape the hustle and bustle of London," Armstrong added. "When I saw him earlier in the week, he said he planned to return to his estate but gave no exact date."

A knock sounded at the door, and then Jenkins entered the

room, holding his nose.

"Why are you holding your nose, Jenkins?" Lady Beadle asked.

"You'll find out," Jenkins murmured before announcing, "Lord Wilton has arrived."

A moment later, Michael entered the room. "Stanhope, my butler, said there was a fire, my lady," he said, scanning the room with a look of confusion.

"Well done, Jenkins. I declare you are a mind reader, for you have once again anticipated our needs," Lady Beadle said with a grin. "Now then, Lord Wilton—Michael, thank you for coming."

"Of course, Lady Beadle, I am at your service."

Lady Beadle gave a firm nod. "Yes, there was a fire. My solicitor's home was burned down, apparently by an arsonist. His sister-in-law, Lady Emma Grantham, and her niece fled here for safety. We must help them." She wrinkled her nose. "Good Lord! My ears are working with this ear horn, but my eyes are watering, and my nose… What is that *smell?*"

Michael sighed and leaned on his cane. "I apologize. It's a salve that Hastings insisted I use on my leg. I had hoped I could do it without notice...but I received your missive and came immediately."

Lady Beadle waved away the apology. "Never you mind. I've smelled far worse. Besides, the pungent scent does nothing to detract from your charm, my dear. You're still the most handsome man in London."

Emma, who was sitting next to Celia, was unable to get a good glimpse of Lord Wilton because Armstrong had stood to greet him.

But the earl's rich, deep baritone made her heart skip a beat—although she couldn't for the life of her figure out why.

"Come, come," Lady Beadle said a few minutes later, thumping her cane on the carpet as the two men spoke in hushed tones. "You can discuss the investigation after we make the introductions."

Emma could still not catch a decent glimpse of Lord Wilton, but then Armstrong stepped aside, fully revealing the earl. Her breath caught in her throat at the man standing before her.

"Lord Michael Wilton, allow me to introduce you to Lady Emma Grantham," Lady Beadle said with a smile as though she were presiding over the opening ball of the London Season.

He was the most handsome man Emma had ever seen. His blond hair curled about his head like Apollo, the god of the sun in Greek mythology. His striking green eyes reminded her of the color of the sea, clear, deep, and endless. It was as if he had stepped right out of a painting. She blinked, wondering if she was dreaming.

The blond Adonis appeared befuddled as he regarded Emma, and she worried that he might not be amenable to the idea of her and Katie staying at his estate. But then he smiled—and bent over her hand.

Lord, what a smile.

"Lady Grantham, it is a pleasure to meet you. Allow me to offer my home to you and your niece for as long as you need it," he said in that rich baritone that almost made her swoon.

"Thank you, my lord, for offering to help us," Emma said, realizing that Armstrong must have quickly explained the situation during their quiet exchange. "But I will accept no charity. I must insist on working for our keep."

CHAPTER FOUR

Just before sunrise
On a road somewhere, heading to Sussex

MY GOD! SHE'S *captivating, and she's the most stubborn woman I've ever met,* Michael mused, his gaze fixed on Lady Emma Grantham, seated across from him in the carriage. Her niece, Katie, was nestled beside her, with Doris—the maid Lady Beadle had insisted accompany them—leaning against the carriage wall.

The soft glow of morning filtered through the window, catching the red-gold strands in Emma's hair and casting a warm halo around her. Even in slumber, she was beautiful. And those eyes—those extraordinary violet eyes—had regarded him earlier with a frankness he wasn't used to in a woman, save for his sister, Lady Beadle, and the wives of his closest friends. She was exhausted—he could see it in the paleness of her cheeks, the faint rasp in her smoke-roughened voice—but still carried herself with quiet dignity, insisting she would be no burden. She would absolutely not be a burden, no, but the woman was as hardheaded as they came.

Katie, curled against her aunt's side, looked angelic in sleep, and even Doris, who protested at first about riding in a carriage before breakfast, had dozed off within moments of their departure, her snores growing louder with every mile.

A fond smile crept over his lips in quiet amusement as he recalled the spirited exchanges with Emma—her adamant refusal to accept charity, and her resolve to take up the housekeeper's role on her terms. He exhaled slowly, the amusement fading into a heaviness he couldn't shake.

She'll be dangerous to have around, he reminded himself. Too bright. Too direct. She was a wild card in a game he no longer wished to play. The war had altered him in ways he still didn't fully understand. Once he had dreamed of eagerly taking a wife, having children—a home filled with laughter. But now all that remained were scars—deep and jagged, carved into his skin, others buried deep, scars he would never inflict on another. He could not—*would not*—let any woman see the darkness he carried deep in his soul.

Ultimately, he had given in, but privately, he wished he had arrived *before* Lady Beadle suggested the position. He would have offered Emma and Katie sanctuary at his estate without any mention of employment. It felt awkward, even improper, to have a lady, and that lady in particular, serving as his housekeeper. But Armstrong had interceded, ever the voice of reason, and convinced him that the arrangement added another layer of protection. A practical disguise, shielding both Emma and the child.

Both Celia and Lady Beadle had agreed with reasoning that echoed Armstrong's advice, that the housekeeper position offered the perfect means of hiding Emma in plain sight. It had been a clever bit of misdirection, and the more Michael had considered it, the more it made sense. It had given him just enough justification to move forward with the plan, at least for now—until the arsonist was identified and brought to justice.

He dragged a hand through his hair and exhaled heavily. It felt as though days had passed since the plan had been discussed— when in truth, it had been scarcely a few hours. Lady Beadle, with her usual persistence, had also insisted that Doris accompany them, both as chaperone and as personal maid. Emma had protested at first, pointing out that she had no need of a lady's maid, particularly as she was to serve as Michael's housekeeper.

But this time it was Celia's gentle wisdom that persuaded her. Doris would be a great help with Katie, especially while Emma was busy with her new duties.

Lady Beadle had added that Katie had already taken a liking to Doris. The maid possessed an uncanny ability for putting young visitors at ease, ensuring they wanted for nothing during their stay. Her cheerful nature and lighthearted laughter had a way of making even the most mundane moments feel joyful—something Michael suspected would be no small comfort to a child who'd just lost her home.

Emma had retired to rest for a few hours while the four of them—Michael, Armstrong, Lady Celia, and Lady Beadle—remained in the drawing room to finalize the details of how best to move Lady Emma and Katie, without drawing attention. The plan that took shape was not unlike others he and Armstrong had devised in the past during their more covert endeavors.

"How do you plan to move Emma and Katie?" Lady Beadle had asked, not one to mince words. "I know you boys are experts at all this espionage business but humor an old woman and explain what you have in mind."

"First, we generally review all the possible options, Aunt Millie," Armstrong replied. "But given that time is of the essence, the goal is to move them without anyone noticing. Think of it like that sleight-of-hand trick we saw at the Adelphi. Remember? One moment, the conjurer was holding your fan—and the next, it had disappeared."

Lady Beadle's brow arched. "Yes. My most prized fan. French ivory, hand-painted silk. And where did it reappear?" Her lips twitched. "In the vicar's coat pocket. I thought the poor man was going to faint, so scandalized he was when the magician asked him to look inside. Bright red, he went."

Armstrong and Michael had exchanged an amused glance with Celia, who lifted her teacup to hide her smile.

"I saw him a few days later at Lady Farnsworth's tea," Lady Beadle added. "He turned crimson all over again when I asked after his rheumatism. Poor man. I imagine he's still recovering."

"So, the idea is to create a bit of misdirection—spirit Emma and Katie away without anyone noticing," Armstrong said.

"We should leave very early in the morning, when no one is expecting us to depart," Michael added.

"By *anyone*, you mean the arsonist," Lady Beadle said, her tone shrewd.

Both men had nodded.

Emma now stirred in her sleep, shifting slightly as the carriage jostled along the rutted road. A loose curl slipped across her cheek, obscuring her face.

Michael hesitated. Then, almost without thinking, he leaned forward and gently tucked the lock behind her ear. His fingers brushed her skin—soft, warm—and he immediately sat back, frowning at himself.

She and Katie had been through a harrowing night. They needed protection. They needed to feel safe again. And most of all, they needed rest.

He dragged a hand through his hair again, a habit he'd never quite shaken when something unsettled him. Turning to stare out the window, he pushed aside the strange knot in his chest. *Focus, damn it.*

His thoughts returned to the conversation from just hours earlier...

"It's important to get them out of town, Aunt Millie—away from the arsonist," Armstrong had said, ever the pragmatist. "He wouldn't be expecting them to leave again so soon—if he even followed them here. And unless he shows himself, we can't be sure he saw them arrive at your house."

"They can rest in the carriage on the way to Sussex," Michael added. "I doubt Lady Grantham will have the energy or focus to do much today. Tonight's given her quite a shock."

"But if the arsonist knows who she is, it's the last place he'd think to look—and with the route we're taking by road, it should take about a day and a half to reach Sussex," Michael continued.

"But if we use the river and take it part of the way, we can cut the time in half."

"Emma knows her mind. She's not made of fluff, as so many Society girls are today. She does not shirk hard work," Lady Beadle explained. "Besides, with all that's happened, the girl needs to stay busy. And…I want to make sure she stays well. This is an arsonist, for God's sake."

"We'll take every precaution, Aunt Millie," Armstrong assured her. "We'll use unmarked carriages along with some sleight of hand, such as entering the front of an inn, only to walk out the back and get into a different carriage, changing clothing, and using rural back roads and a light rig. If someone is tailing us, we'll make damn sure they lose the trail and be unable to guess our destination."

Michael had smiled then, recalling the gleam in the dowager's eyes. For a moment, he could've sworn she was plotting to join them herself.

He was glad that Hastings, Stanhope, and Mrs. McDonald had planned to follow later in the day—leaving just a skeleton staff at the townhouse, he had informed Lady Beadle. "If we've forgotten anything," he'd told her, "Send it along with them. They'll be taking the direct route and should arrive well ahead of us."

The carriage lurched as one of the wheels struck a rut in the road, jarring Michael from his thoughts. The plan, the secrecy, the familiar rhythm of covert strategy—all of it faded as the present reasserted itself.

He glanced at his pocket watch. They would reach The Rooster's Inn in a couple of hours, he estimated, leaning back against the leather squabs…

He took some comfort in knowing Armstrong was nearby, accompanied by several outriders positioned to watch the road behind them. If the arsonist had followed, Michael felt confident they'd spot him.

Still, he kept his eyes sharp, scanning the terrain through the window, alert to anything unusual.

The last time he and Armstrong pulled off this sort of operation had been years ago, while smuggling a French marquis through England to a safe house in Cornwall. The man had turned informant, offering intelligence on an imminent insurrection in exchange for sanctuary. Thanks to his information, they'd been able to prevent what would have become a bloody and widespread protest.

This mission was different. But the stakes were no less personal.

The main objective today was to avoid the major coaching roads, particularly the turnpike, which would have tollgates and far more people who might be able to recall seeing them, should someone ask. Instead, they would cut across Kent into Sussex, keeping to rural back roads through the countryside and passing through small villages. At least, that was what this carriage would be doing. If things worked out the way Michael and Armstrong planned, he, Emma, Katie, and Doris would be on a more direct route, using the Thames as much as possible.

His manor, Wilton Hall, was in the South Downs region, an area known for its rolling chalk hills, wooded valleys, and sweeping vistas of open grassland. There was sea access nearby and a comforting sense of seclusion. It was far enough from London to provide peace, yet close enough when duty—or Society—called.

He had visited the estate twice since inheriting the title. Structurally, it was sound. But the interior would need considerable work—fresh paint, new furnishings, and improvements to the overgrown grounds. A slow, steady project.

Michael's gaze drifted across the carriage once more. Lady Emma slept quietly beside her niece, her expression softened in slumber. He wondered if she'd be content with the role of housekeeper—especially when the bulk of the work ahead would involve overseeing the refurbishment of a neglected estate.

She didn't strike him as a woman who feared a challenge.

At one time, Wilton Hall had been known for its horse breeding. Since learning of his inheritance, Michael had been considering it as a possible future pursuit for himself—something tangible, methodical. The stables offered plenty of space, though they'd require substantial repair before any horses could be properly housed. Still, it was a project he found himself looking forward to. The stable had plenty of space, but it would need a lot of repairs before the stable could be used—and this was a project that he looked forward to undertaking.

A soft murmur drew his attention. Emma shifted against the squabs in her sleep, and the sight of her—peaceful, unaware— stirred something unexpected in him.

Her hair, rich with copper tones, shimmered in the shifting morning light, and it irritated him more than he cared to admit that he found it beautiful. That he found *her* beautiful. And those eyes—lavender with curious flecks of gold—had a way of meeting his with a startling frankness. As if she saw far more than he intended to reveal.

But he would keep his distance. He had to.

With young Katie in her care and the responsibilities awaiting her at the estate, Emma would be kept busy. And so would he. Michael would be able to keep his distance. There was no way he would allow himself to become involved, no matter how attractive she was. He was too damaged for any woman.

HE STOOD SILENTLY in the shadows across from Curzon Street. His broad-brimmed black hat was pulled low to obscure his face, and his long coat shrouded him in darkness. Lights flickered intermittently in the upper windows of the townhouse, but it was the steady glow in the center of the house that held his attention. That was where she was—*her*, the woman who had intrigued him and lured him into this desolation.

The house had buzzed with activity for hours. And as dawn crept closer, he became increasingly certain this was where she'd gone. He had intended to set her home alight, watch it burn until nothing remained. He'd thought it would bring peace. That elusive peace.

It hadn't.

Now, he understood.

He didn't want peace.

He wanted *her*.

A distant sound broke into his thoughts. A carriage rolled in from the mews behind the house, slowed, and turned onto the cobbled street, pushing him deeper into the shadows. Its black-lacquered sides glinted briefly before it disappeared around the corner.

Moments later, another carriage emerged—but turned in the opposite direction.

Too dark to make out the lettering on either side. But he knew—*she* was in one of them.

And he would find her.

Satisfied that neither carriage had seen him, he stepped out from the shadows and untied his horse from the mulberry bush. As he mounted, he paused only briefly before nudging the animal toward the first carriage's route, keeping far enough behind to remain unseen.

But not too far.

He had a job to finish.

CHAPTER FIVE

ROUSED BY THE din of the carriage rolling down the dirt-covered road, Emma opened her eyes just enough to see Michael through the fringe of her lashes. His eyes were closed, and he appeared to be sleeping. The gaslight in the carriage was dim, with heavy black velvet curtains drawn. She lifted the corner of the curtain and saw it was still dark. *How long have I been asleep?*

Despite her continued agitation over the fire and the grogginess of just waking, Emma found it difficult to ignore the undeniable attractiveness of the man seated across from her. Then there was that adorable dimple etched into his lower-right chin, and thick, blonde, curly hair that curled over his collar. Although longer than what was fashionable for men, the length gave him a rakish air that suited him. It contrasted strikingly with his masculine face, especially the rugged cut of his square jaw. Not to mention his tall, broad-shouldered frame. Truth be told, everything about Michael made Emma's heart race.

"You're awake," he whispered, the low rumble of his voice taking her by surprise. His captivating green eyes, now open, seemed to twinkle in the dim glow of the gas lamp.

He caught me. The thought that he may have been watching her made her feel both self-conscious and flattered at the same time. And something else—*safe.* She'd had barely enough time to comb her hair and wash her face before they departed. She had hastily changed into a clean gown, one of the few that she'd managed to stuff into her valise before she and Katie made their escape from the burning home. Well, it couldn't be helped. She had the pouch with the household funds that she'd retrieved from Martin's study. It wasn't much, but it should enable her to purchase a few necessities and perhaps some simple muslin or cotton to make gowns for herself and Katie.

"If you're up to it, I want to review our plan to get you and Katie safely to my estate. There are a few things concerning you and her that you'll need to know. Everything is already in motion. Armstrong and I have already begun to execute it."

"Lord Wilton, do you think the arsonist is following us?" she said, alarm coursing through her. She hugged her niece closer, twirling her fingers through the soft brown curls. The child was still in a deep sleep. Thankfully, she hadn't stirred since they'd left Lady Beadle's.

"You agreed to call me Michael when we were at Lady Beadle's. As far as his following us… That is what we hope to prevent," he said in a measured tone. "He knows you have seen him—both you and Katie—so we need to do the utmost to make sure to protect the two of you and to catch him before he can wreak more havoc."

She gave a nod. "So, what *is* the plan, Michael?" she asked, testing his name on her lips. She glanced to her right and noticed Doris hadn't stirred either.

"We are an hour or so outside of London and will be arriving at an inn soon, giving the impression that we will be checking in for the night. But in truth, you and Katie will change into disguises and then we will leave through the rear exit, assisted by the innkeeper and his wife."

"What sort of disguises?"

"Boys' clothing. You and Katie will dress as a youth and his young brother," he said before clearing his throat.

His discomfort was not lost on Emma. "Boys' clothing?"

"Yes, you're too petite of stature to pass for the average man, so once disguised, you'll resemble an older boy traveling with his young brother. We need to make sure your identity is disguised, in case we're being followed. Remember, the appearance will be that you are staying at the inn for the night. As lovely as you are, you will be noticed leaving the inn. If the arsonist is following us, he will ask…and someone will recall. But no one will likely notice a scruffy urchin and his equally scruffy little brother," Michael explained.

As lovely as you are…?

Did she just hear correctly?

She felt a blush heat her cheeks. She hoped he couldn't see it in the dimly lit interior of the carriage.

She watched his lips move as he spoke. Perhaps it was just her fatigue, but she couldn't help it. She couldn't recall being fascinated by a man as she was by the earl.

Pay attention, you ninny. And stop acting like a besotted debutante at her first ball.

Katie's safety depended upon her. She needed to pay attention.

"We will approach it like dressing up, with Katie. She enjoys that," Emma said. A knot formed in her chest as she recalled the times she had played dress-up with Katie at home. Her niece had loved playing the lady of the manor, wearing one of Evie's gowns and one of Emma's hats.

Home.

She gave a brief shake of her head to clear it. That life was behind them now—certainly for the foreseeable future. As long as the arsonist was out there, they would be in danger.

"Good. That helps. Do you think Katie would hide in a trunk, one with holes drilled in it?" he asked.

"No," she whispered, shaking her head. "Katie is terrified of the boogeyman. I'm afraid this whole thing, the fire, will make it worse. But I can carry her…"

"I see," he said, scratching the scruff of his beard. "I think perhaps this calls for a slight change of plan. I will carry Katie, dressed as a little boy, beneath my greatcoat. Her hair will be stuffed beneath a cap. If anyone asks, no one will recall having seen a little girl. She must not speak. This is most important. Can you get her to be quiet?"

Emma nodded. "I can. Where will we be going after we leave the inn?"

The earl leaned forward, close enough that she could smell the appealingly fresh sandalwood scent that seemed to be embedded in his skin.

"Once we leave the inn, another carriage will take us to the Thames, where we will board a swift boat and travel to Sussex, where we will be met by a post-chaise that will take us to my estate. My estate is in Sussex. Depending on the traffic on the river, the journey on the Thames should take approximately five hours. It is the fastest way for us to travel. And it fits well with our plan of subterfuge. Our carriage—this carriage—will continue along the same main thoroughfare, tomorrow morning...but with Armstrong and two outriders, in case it's followed. It's Armstrong's carriage, so eventually, it will return to his estate, and they will be careful not to lead the arsonist anywhere near *my* estate. Additionally, two of Armstrong's guards will join us on the swift boat," he added.

"What if the arsonist catches on to the plan and recognizes us?" A shiver quaked through her. "I can still see his face in my mind." She could *never* forget his face.

"We will know if he attempts to follow us, or if he's hired someone to do so. Trust me. You and Katie, and Doris must do as I say and follow the plan—we should be halfway to Sussex before anyone notices that we did not stay the night at the inn. The point is to blend in—hide in plain sight."

"What is Doris's disguise?" she asked, biting back a smile.

"The sleepy chaperone will remain the same. She's perfect as she is," he said, his lips twitching.

Emma smiled. "Yes. Doris is so biddable and cheerful...but she did fall asleep five minutes into our trip."

"She's like so many lady's maids. She'll be wonderful—especially with Katie," Lord Wilton concurred.

A few minutes later, the carriage rolled off the main road onto the gravel drive that led to the Red Rooster Inn.

"Wake up, Katie darling," Emma said, jostling her niece awake.

"Auntie…Emma," Katie whispered, sleep slurring her words. "Are we there yet?"

"Not quite, my darling. Lord Wilton and Lord Armstrong have conceived a clever plan to make sure the bad man can't find us. It will be great fun, like a little game. Something you love"

"Oh, I love games," Katie said, with a wide smile. "Will Mama and Papa be there?"

"Soon…we will see them as soon as possible, I promise," Emma said, making a mental note to find out how Evie would find them. Katie needed her mother. "And we will be playing dress-up."

"I like dressing up. Can I be a sailor?" Emma asked.

"Yes…in a sense. You will be a little boy, but we will need to be very quiet. We will have a contest to see which of us can be the quietest, once we are dressed up," Emma explained.

"You will dress up too?" Katie asked.

"I will…" Emma smiled. "I'll be a boy, too!"

"Oh, what fun," Katie said. "I hope I win. What will I win?"

"What if I surprise you?" Emma asked, smiling at the little girl. She could always count on Katie.

"I like surprises even more," Katie said, her eyes dancing with mischief.

"Good girl," Emma said, hugging her close. "We're ready," she said, turning to the handsome earl seated across from her. Though she had to stop thinking of him that way. He would be her *employer*. She would be his housekeeper.

Talk about playing dress-up, she thought sardonically.

"Will he be dressing up?" Katie asked, looking in Lord Wilton's direction.

"No, but he will be carrying you. We must do as he says…but remember the contest. We must be quiet as mice," Emma instructed her.

Katie nodded, her eyes sparkling with excitement.

Doris sneezed and opened her eyes, appearing slightly disoriented.

"That's an odd way to wake up," Emma said, smiling at the older woman. "Are you all right?"

"Oh, it's just the damp air. Traveling always does this to me," Doris said, taking out a handkerchief and blowing her nose.

"We have arrived at the Red Rooster Inn," Lord Wilton said. "Here's the plan, Doris. We will check into the inn and then leave silently through the rear exit after Lady Emma and Katie don disguises as boys."

"Do you think we've been followed?" the maid asked. "Lady Beadle said I needed to watch for anything unusual and let you know if I saw someone."

Emma's lips twitched as she recalled Lord Wilton's name for Doris…*the sleepy chaperone.* "Did you see anyone?" she asked.

Doris shook her head. "Er, not that I recall. However, I shall be more diligent from now on."

Emma squeezed her shoulder. "It's all right, dear Doris. Lord Armstrong and Lord Wilton have thought of everything. Hopefully, we will be safely at Lord Wilton's estate before anyone notices we are no longer there."

"Do you think we are being followed?" Doris asked, her breath hitching.

"We won't know for a little while yet," Lord Wilton said.

"We're going to play dress-up!" Katie announced proudly.

"Oh! Do I have a part?" Doris asked.

"Yes. You will be as you are, the maid, but there will be no lines to say," Lord Wilton said. The carriage stopped under the awning near the entrance. "Everyone ready?" he asked.

"Ready!" Katie said with a little hop.

"Very good. Remember the plan. Follow me and remember

not to speak. I must talk to the innkeeper first. Then you'll be donning your disguise, and then we'll be going down the back stairs and leaving through a door in the back of the inn," he said, picking up a valise by his feet.

As they entered the inn, a short, pudgy, bespectacled man, who identified himself as Mr. Kirk, the innkeeper, met them. He looked around and then lowered his voice to a whisper. "This is m'wife, m'lord," he said, indicating a woman next to him, who seemed to appear out of the air. "We have a room upstairs ready for your party. Your room is the first door to the right. And when you are ready, we stand ready to assist."

"Thank you, Mr. Kirk," Lord Wilton said, gripping the valise and checking the inside, before placing a gold sovereign in the innkeeper's hand. "I take it Lord Armstrong has already arrived?"

"Yes, he is in the tavern. You will be leaving through the back door. He will see you there."

Lord Wilton turned to Emma. "Ladies, and Katie, here is your key. First door to the right. Doris, here's a brown valise to pack Emma and Katie's clothing in. You will need to carry it down. Leave nothing behind. I'll be here waiting. Be as quick as you can."

"Yes, my lord," Doris said, taking the key.

The three of them went upstairs—Emma holding Katie's hand—leaving Lord Wilton with the innkeeper. As she reached the top of the stairs, Emma glanced over her shoulder, and her eyes met Lord Wilton's as he gave her an encouraging nod.

Lord William Armstrong nodded at Wilton as they passed each other in the small hallway at the bottom of the back stairs. Wilton gave him a nod and touched his left brow, a signal they had agreed on to mean all was going to plan. Mr. Kirk had become an experienced and trusted resource, someone they had depended on for this type of escape on several occasions. Pleased, Armstrong took a sip of his drink. Keeping his black hat pulled low over his face, he stepped outside and watched Wilton's group leave in the black post-chaise waiting for them with two of his outriders. They would arrive at the Thames in two hours and board the boat that was waiting for them.

Dressed as a disheveled, unshaven older man, Armstrong took his seat near the back of the tavern, a place that gave him an excellent view of his surroundings.

The innkeeper's wife checked to make sure Lady Grantham, Doris, and Katie had left behind nothing that could betray their identities. "Here's your mug of ale, m'lord," she said, setting down the beverage. "Now drink up and begone with you. You're stinking up the place." That was code for *everything went like clockwork*.

As he took a new seat in a corner closer to the door, he watched and waited for his quarry. He wasn't disappointed.

"May I speak with the innkeeper?" a tall man demanded of the innkeeper's wife. His brimmed hat was low over his face as he stepped up to the bar.

Armstrong studied the man, feeling there was something familiar about him, but unable to pinpoint what it was. The man's head was partially hidden beneath the brim. It irritated him that he couldn't see the man's face. The only thing he could make out was a long, thin, aristocratic nose.

"Yes, m'lord?" Mr. Kirk said, emerging from a back room and hanging his apron on a hook behind the bar. "I understand you wish to see me."

"I'm looking for a woman and child—a girl. My wife and child." The man cleared his throat. "They were just ahead of me, and I lost them. I was to have met them here before they departed. Unfortunately, I was delayed. Have you seen them?"

Mr. Kirk's expression was one of pure puzzlement. "No, m'lord. Ye know we don't typically have children in an establishment such as this. Not good for business, you know."

Armstrong lifted the brim of his hat slightly to better see the man's face, but his effort was met by disappointment. Even so, the man's voice and stature seemed familiar.

"I'll ask my wife. Betty, come here," Mr. Kirk called, beckoning the woman who, five minutes earlier, had disappeared into the kitchen.

Mrs. Kirk emerged from the kitchen, carrying a tray with a pot of tea, two teacups, and a plate of biscuits. She set the tray down on the counter of the bar. "Yes, husband? You called?"

"Wife, this gentleman has a question," Mr. Kirk said, patting his wife on the shoulder. "We must try to help him."

"Have you seen a woman and a small girl?" the man demanded again. "They are my wife and child, and I am trying to catch up to them before they get too far. We are meant to visit my parents in Kent, and I am worried about them traveling alone. I was delayed on a business matter in London and planned to meet them here. Alas, I seem to have missed their departure."

Mrs. Kirk looked up at her husband, giving a horrified look. "Good heavens, no, m'lord!" She waved her hand around the tavern at the various ruffians and drunkards, all leaning into their tankards and looking like baths only happened at the point of a gun. "We are not the sort of establishment that would 'ave children in our tavern."

"A yes or no is sufficient," the man replied, clearly annoyed. "You're certain they haven't come through?" He held out a small purse. "It could be worth your while to help me."

"We're certain, aren't we, Betty?" Mr. Kirk feigned interest in the purse, reaching out to hold it.

Mrs. Kirk gave a quick nod and smiled. "Yes, husband. We are certain. 'Tis such a rarity to see a child stay here. Why, it's been nigh on three summers since the last child stayed here. Don't you recall? It was storming, and the father's carriage wheel broke, and he and his young son had no place to go."

"Yes, wife. I recall that, now that you mention it," Mr. Kirk agreed.

Mrs. Kirk looked at the stranger. "I'm sorry, m'lord, but

we've seen no young woman or girl. We'd certainly know if they were here."

After squeezing the small sack of coins, Mr. Kirk returned it. "It's a goodly sum, m'lord, and I dearly wish we could help. But we 'aven't seen yer wife and child." He tapped his chin. "There *was* a carriage about an hour ago that changed horses. I didn't see who was inside, as the transaction was with my stable."

"Describe the carriage," the man demanded.

"Oh dear!" Mrs. Kirk muttered. "I wish I could remember… But I didn't realize we'd be questioned about it later. I'm very sorry, m'lord."

"Let me take care of this, my dear," Mr. Kirk muttered, stepping in front of her. "Black, no markings. I only noticed it because the driver wanted black horses, and we had exactly four to switch. Strange request, don't you think?"

Good job, Kirk, Armstrong thought, amused at the man's ingenuity and his lengthy explanations. The Kirks' extensive discussion seemed to irritate the arsonist and unsettle him. The innkeeper and his wife had assisted Wilton and Armstrong numerous times over the past year. Not only was Mr. Kirk paid by Armstrong, but the Crown always gave a sizable token of appreciation for those businesses that aided in cases.

Once the arsonist left, Armstrong slid from behind the table and followed him, keeping to the dark side of the building. He watched him get into an older carriage, a black conveyance with red paint on its wheel rims. Could it have been stolen? There was also the question of why Mr. Kirk and his wife referred to the man as *m'lord*. What was it that would have led them to treat him as a member of the aristocracy? People in their positions rarely made that sort of mistake. Did they recognize him? Perhaps it was the man's manner of speaking or his attire; he was dressed in a greatcoat and hat, as was Armstrong. Before leaving, he intended to ask for more details.

Still, he had an eerie sense that he'd met the arsonist somewhere before…but where and when?

CHAPTER SIX

A S THE FOUR stepped from the carriage, Emma noticed the outriders from Lord Armstrong's security move through the shadows, toward the wharf. From the corner of her eye, she caught the slight nod Michael gave them. Knowing they were part of their group made her feel safer, especially since the arsonist was somewhere and she had no idea *where*.

Emma looked down at her niece and squeezed her tightly against her. "Sweetheart, I need to remind you—if anyone speaks to us, you must remember we will nod but not speak. Going to the wharf, we need to conduct ourselves exactly as we did at the tavern. Can we do it?"

"I can, Auntie. I promise," Katie said.

Emma glanced at Doris, who had grown quiet. "Doris, how are you feeling?"

"I've been able to catch a few winks, my lady," Doris said. "I feel rested."

Emma bit her tongue. Every time she glanced Doris's way, the older woman was asleep and snoring.

Behind her, Lord Wilton cleared his throat. "Ladies, we're at the Thames. Do you think we can do this? Get to the pier without incident?"

"I do. Katie's tired and will probably fall asleep on the boat— the sooner we get on the boat, the sooner we'll be at our new home."

Lord Wilton smiled. "There are a lot of regulars here, and we don't want anyone to know that a lady and a little girl came through. They must think you are boys. It's nice to think that the manor house could be a real home. It's nothing less than what this one deserves," he said, nodding at Katie.

Finding their way through the men on the wharf proved easy enough. Lively chatter from the seamen in the area offered a convenient background as they slipped around the groups of people with ease.

Within what seemed like minutes, Doris, Emma, and Katie were safely aboard a boat and on their way down the Thames. The craft, carved from pine, resembled a slender fish gliding effortlessly through the waves. Its elongated frame was perfect for cutting through the murky river water, shrouded by a thick blanket of fog.

⇶⟫⟪⇷

MICHAEL STOOD AT the rail of the boat, next to his friend, Wright. Wright was speaking to one of his men while Michael studied the traffic pattern on the Thames. Even with darkness upon them, boats of all sizes floated alongside the outside edges of the river. Their boat was in the center, moving at a faster clip than most of the other, smaller boats that surrounded them.

He studied the small cutter they were on, glad that Wright had joined them. The boat was long, lean, and shallow. Two weathered watermen, sitting side by side, fluidly moved two long oars through the water, rhythmically slicing through the surface while periodically taking orders from Wright as they maneuvered the craft past other boats and rafts scattered along the Thames. From the back, Armstrong's two guards, who'd been waiting for them when they arrived, scanned the area around them, looking for any sign that they had been followed.

Michael could see men moving on the shores of the Thames, but with the dim light provided, he couldn't see more than their shadowed figures. With nothing to see there, he allowed his mind to wander back to when they first arrived at the boat, the first few minutes of boarding, when his friend had turned his attention to Emma, creating a familiar irritation—one he was used to dealing with when Wright and beautiful women occupied the same room.

Emma kissed Katie's forehead and let her look around with Doris as she approached the railing next to Michael. "I'm glad to have finally made it to the boat. It's been a long day. The plan went off smoothly. Did you plan all of this—all from London?" she'd asked, her eyes glittering with excitement as she looked from Michael to Wright.

Michael smiled. "I'm glad you think it's working well, Lady Emma. The main thing is to get you and Katie to safety. But no. I didn't plan it all. It was a team effort."

Wright cleared his throat. "Will I be getting an introduction?" he asked his friend.

"Certainly. Allow me to introduce Lady Emma Grantham. Emma, this is Viscount Asher H. Wright, a friend of mine," Michael replied.

"It's nice to meet you, Lady Emma," Wright said, taking her hand and gently kissing it.

A sharp, twisting sensation pierced Michael's chest, like a knife carving into his heart. Adding to this irritation, his pulse sped up. Despite his taking a calming breath, the rapid pulse wouldn't quite subside, and he was certain it was a response to what was going on around him. Wright had wasted no time in enchanting Emma, even as she had still been dressed as a boy. Although his best friend had vowed never to marry, Wright began to charm Emma, something of a routine when he was with the ladies.

"You were right about her, Michael," Wright said, picking up Emma's hand and turning it in his, looking her in the eye. "My lady, you're pulling off this ruse with little trouble—although now that I have realized you are a lady, and a beautiful one at that, I cannot unsee your beauty. I fear it shall be impossible for me to ignore your presence," he

said before directing one of his men to show Emma, Katie, and Doris to the small cabin where they could rest. Wright's charm with women had always been so effortless.

The irritation that pulsed through Michael puzzled him. They were in a race to get to his manor house before being discovered by the arsonist, and he kept replaying this scene in his mind, almost clouding it from anything else. Wright's flirtatious ways had never irritated him thus.

When he glanced at Emma, he noticed her face had turned a lovely shade of pink, illuminated by the yellow-tinged lantern light, and felt a sinking feeling. The irritation this time felt different—more personal.

Was this—could this truly be—jealousy? The thought was foreign and unsettling. He had never been a jealous person. He felt possessiveness, a feeling he hadn't felt since he was ten and reluctantly had to share his beloved pony with his cousin, a memory he had long since buried. The intensity of his feelings surprised Michael and stirred a whirlwind of confusion. They were friends.

He gave his head a slight shake, as if to clear it and wipe the thoughts away.

Michael had begun to think of Wright more like a brother since they had met nearly a year ago. The man was always the first one to show up to help, always willing to lend a hand. No amount of money could ever reflect the value of his life, which Wright had helped save. Michael would surely have perished in the cave where they found him. He had been beaten, starved, tied to a chair, and left to drown as high tide rushed in—and Michael had been too weak to do much to save himself.

When Wright and his friend, Edward Sinclair, found Michael in the cave, he had been suffering from what could have been fatal wounds. Yet he had been saved by men he had never met before, who would go on to become his best friends and most trusted allies.

Wright and Baron Edward Sinclair had taken him to the home of Lord and Lady Matthew Romney to heal. Lady Bethany Romney, an American who had saved Matthew's life during the

Battle of New Orleans, had been trained in herbal healing. Her efforts were instrumental in saving Michael's life. The only outward sign of his injuries was his limp—something he still had difficulty acknowledging.

As he wrestled with his frustrations, Emma appeared from the small cabin, seeming more refreshed.

"Katie and Doris are sleeping," she said, smiling. "Doris fell asleep almost immediately. Katie needed a bedtime story."

"They were both so exhausted, they could barely keep their eyes open," Michael said, smiling. "My bet is the sleepy chaperone and your niece will sleep until we arrive in Gravesend. Once the boat arrives at the port in Gravesend, then it could take another hour's carriage ride—maybe longer, depending on traffic and conditions—before we arrive at Wilton House."

"It's a welcome relief after the long carriage ride to be able to stand and move about," she said. She looked around at the river and then up at Michael. "Everything has moved so quickly on this trip."

"Yes, it has," Michael said. She needed some sleep. He felt like a cad for not immediately encouraging her to rest. But throughout the trip, he had begun to realize that he enjoyed having her near, conversing with her. He was astonished that it had taken him until *this* moment to appreciate her beauty. "I wish it didn't have to be this way, but we needed to act swiftly to create confusion with the arsonist and to get you and Katie to safety."

"Yes, I understand," Emma said. "I am so grateful to you and to Lord Wright and Lord Armstrong for everything you've done."

"You are most welcome," Wright said with a smile as he approached. "It has been my pleasure to assist in any way that I can."

Michael cleared his throat, irritated once again by the charming smile Wright gave Emma—and her answering smile. "It's been a long day, Lady Emma, and I am certain you are exhausted," he said. "We have about five hours before we arrive at

Gravesend. Perhaps you should retire to the cabin and get some sleep."

Emma nodded. "I think you're right. I could use a couple of hours to rest my eyes."

The sound of the cabin door opening drew their attention, and they turned to see Katie stepping onto the deck, her doll clutched to her chest.

"Katie, what are you doing awake?" Emma asked, rushing over to her and picking her up.

"Doris rolled over and I fell off the bed," Katie said, wiping at the sleep in her eyes.

Emma and Michael looked at each other, exchanging a smile at the child's admission.

"Are you hurt, princess?" Michael asked.

Katie shook her head. "Polly got a little squished, but she's all right now."

"Polly is as strong as you are," Michael said.

"Doris falls asleep really fast, Auntie," Katie said, clutching her aunt's dress. "She didn't even wake up when I did. I tried to get her to wake up, but she just rolled over, and that's when I fell off the bed."

Michael wondered if there was more to the mishap. "Katie, did you by chance have a bad dream?" he asked.

She nodded. "The bad man from the fire was chasing me and Polly. I yelled for Auntie Emma, but she wasn't there. No matter how much I yelled for help, no one came," Katie whispered, her lips trembling. She hugged Polly closer.

"Aww, little one," Michael said, reaching out to touch her cheek gently with the back of his hand. "Dreams can be scary, but talking about the bad ones helps make you feel better."

"I do feel better," Katie said, bobbing her head up and down, seeming to reflect on the advice.

"Good girl. And just so you know, that bad man is far away, and Lord Wright and I are right here—just outside the cabin, making sure no one bothers you," Michael said.

"That's right, sweetness," Wright added. "You have many protectors, like knights in shining armor."

"Really?" Katie said, her eyes wide. "Are you really a knight?"

"Kind of," Wright said softly, tapping the tip of her nose.

"See? You have lots of protectors, including me," Emma added.

Katie smiled and tucked her head on her aunt's shoulder.

"Try to get some more sleep," Michael suggested. "Wright and I will be right here, just a few feet away, keeping watch."

"Just like knights in shining armor?" Katie asked, a hint of mischievousness in her voice.

"Just like knights in shining armor," Michael said with a smile.

Emma placed her finger under Katie's chin. "Are we ready for our adventure?"

"I'm ready, Auntie," Katie said.

"Let's say goodnight to our brave knights."

"Goodnight, brave knights," Katie said with a little wave.

"Thank you," Emma said softly to Michael and Wright, then turned and carried her niece back to the cabin.

"What an enchanting child," Wright said.

Michael heaved a deep sigh. "That she is."

"Have faith, man. If anyone can track down this arsonist, it's Armstrong."

"Yes, I know," Michael said. "I'll be relieved when we get them to the estate, where they'll be safe."

"I understand," Wright said. "And we'll do everything in our power to catch that bastard."

Michael nodded. So far, their journey had been successful, with no mishaps. Once they arrived at his estate, he would ensure that both Emma and Katie felt completely safe and protected. Even though he believed they had done everything to confuse the arsonist as to where they were headed, he wouldn't rest easy until the bastard was caught and hanged for his crimes.

⟫⟫⟫⟪⟪⟪

"STUPID PEOPLE," THE man bit out as he strode from the inn to the carriage. "Liars—the two of them. They think I'm leather-headed." *I'll revisit them sometime in the future, when I have more time to enjoy my retribution.* More than anything, he hated being made a fool of, especially by those he felt were beneath him.

"M-my lord, did you require s-something?" Horace Simms said. Climbing down from the driver's seat, Simms pulled out the step for the older carriage and opened the door for his employer to step up.

"No, Simms. The damnable innkeeper and his foolish wife acted like two lackeys…couldn't get a decent answer from them." *But their day will come,* Viscount Gideon Morgrave thought to himself. As if to seal the idea, he spun around and looked again at the inn, absorbing the setting and the proximity to other buildings—places to sit unseen, that sort of thing—before he turned back to his shabby rented carriage and climbed inside.

"Th-they didn't know where the girl and her daughter went?" Simms said. "A-any instructions?"

"None. But I know she's been here. I can sense it," Morgrave said, his lip curled in a sneer as he looked at the trembling servant. *Damn idiot.* But with his limited funds, it was all he could afford.

"Should we s-search the rooms upstairs?" Simms asked.

"You don't think I haven't thought of that, you simpleton?" Morgrave bit out. "I paid off a maid to check. Dumb chit said there was no one up there matching their descriptions. Total waste of time and coin. She could be anywhere. But I could sense that the innkeeper and his wife were lying to me. Besides, there may have been others spying on me, and I could not afford to allow my appearance to be seen." *Damn! I should have pulled my hat low over my head so that the innkeeper and his wife couldn't get a good look at me.*

"Yes, my lord. Coincidentally, another coach left just as we arrived. I didn't see who was in it, but they seemed in a hurry," Simms offered.

At least you don't have to worry about this one. Simms does as he's told. Weirdly, the thought settled Morgrave. "Was it four black horses?"

"I don't believe so, my lord. The horses looked to be fresh from the stable, prancing and full of energy. There were two brown and two black," Simms replied, his voice shaky. "Shall we try to follow?"

"You're certain only two horses were black?" The damn innkeeper had said *four* were black. "Heading in what direction?"

"Yes, only two horses were black. They turned in the direction of the turnpike, joining a few other carriages that happened by at the same time, but I watched, and it appeared to veer onto a less-traveled road to Kent," Simms replied.

"We'll follow them for a short distance and see if the woman and child are inside. The innkeeper said the carriage had been outfitted with four black horses. Seems a strange thing to lie about." Although he couldn't describe the carriage, except that it was unmarked and black.

"Odd thing. I've been thinking to myself, my lord. The carriage we've been following is taking the back roads, staying off the main road. However, I recall that there was another carriage that left the tavern and turned toward the turnpike, a much busier road." Simms shook his head. "I think we need to take the main road to Kent."

Simms, a man of roughly forty years, stood straighter and relaxed his shoulders. It was a sign of self-confidence Morgrave hadn't seen in the man in years. When Morgrave first met him, it had been in a gaming hell. The man had been in a game with Morgrave, and like Morgrave, he lost. It was one of the many hands Morgrave would lose. He had fallen into drinking and gaming and was addicted to both. Seldom did a night pass when he wasn't gambling somewhere on the East Side of London.

Simms had realized that he was never going to win at cards and opted to leave. But for reasons Morgrave didn't fully understand at the time, he had convinced the man to continue playing. Over cards and drinks that lasted far into the night, and despite both continuing to lose, Simms made a statement to Morgrave that would change both of their lives.

"My lord," he'd said, "we should stop playing. Too many of the new rich are getting richer off our backs. I, for one, cannot afford to allow it. M'wife is threatening to take my daughter and move back to her family's farm. I love my wife, and I promised her I'd change m'ways."

It was when Morgrave realized he had lost his fortune to England's new middle class. These men and women had discovered a niche in trade that met the needs of the *ton*'s wealthy and taken advantage of him. The upper class couldn't work and earn money—it just wasn't done. But the middle class shamelessly made money and, from Morgrave's perspective, dared to encroach upon the events enjoyed by the *ton*. They had taken his fortune, leaving him nearly penniless—except for what he could manage to win. It angered him greatly.

Simms had made a small fortune working for a prominent merchant in town. Unfortunately, he enjoyed gambling, and it seemed he lost at every turn. When Morgrave met the man, he employed him as his driver and footman. Simms was responsible for handling everything Morgrave required, as all the other staff had quit. Over the years, Morgrave had subjected Simms to intimidation, berating him, and threatening his family when things went wrong. Thus, it pleased Morgrave to see that the man was afraid of him; in his mind, this assured him of the man's loyalty.

"Simply trying to throw us off, Simms. I think your first instinct was the best. They're in a hurry, and my guess is they are heading to Kent," Morgrave said. "Let's be on our way."

Simms closed the door, and Morgrave leaned back in the worn leather seat of his coach, frustrated. "No need to overthink this," he murmured, as if assuring himself. *I'm certain they will try to lose us on the busier turnpike. And that's to my advantage. No one will miss her fiery red hair. We'll have an easier time following and getting information.*

He gave a shallow laugh and poured himself a drink from a small satchel next to him before sitting back against the squabs and thinking about the fire. It had been a beautiful thing—almost a cleansing.

The crackling blaze had danced in front of him, its shadows moving in a swirling, hypnotic rhythm. As the fire dwindled to embers and the structure was reduced to a smoldering pile of charred rubble, his attention had turned to the woman...and her fiery hair. Her coppery tresses were exquisite. Never had he seen such beauty. As the surrounding neighbors frantically raised the alarm and attempted to put out the flames, he'd understood he could not let her slip away.

He had lost too much, and now it was time he took what he wanted, relishing the thrill of each scorching conquest. On the night of the fire, he had followed her—something he didn't normally do, for he enjoyed staying behind and watching his masterpieces burn. He enjoyed watching the flames spread and climb, completely consuming everything in their path. But he'd been unable to get the woman and the young girl out of his mind. And so, he'd left the burning house and followed them, staying far enough behind to go unnoticed. Even with two horses, the woman moved too quickly, and he couldn't keep the two of them in his sight, which left him to determine which home had sheltered them. So, he had carefully plotted his course of action, watching and examining each home on Curzon Street. After thoughtful consideration, he was convinced he had identified the right home.

She had eluded him for long enough, but he was determined to find her.

CHAPTER SEVEN

On the boat

A S SHE APPROACHED the cabin, Emma could faintly hear Michael and Wright's voices behind her. Pausing briefly, she turned to glance at the two men who were still engaged in conversation. But the light from an old lantern cast a dim glow and made it difficult to see their faces clearly. Lately, no matter what she was doing, her thoughts drifted to Michael. Perhaps fatigue clouded her mind, but each time she closed her eyes, it was Michael's face she saw.

"The cabin looks small, but I think you'll be able to rest for a few hours," Michael said, coming up behind her and interrupting her thoughts.

"Thank you, Michael. That would be most welcome," Emma said, turning to smile at him, before leading Katie down a few stairs and stepping into the cabin. She wasn't disappointed. The small cabin sat low in the boat, its presence almost unseen from outside. A feather mattress sat on a wooden bunk with what her nose detected to be clean sheets and blankets covering it.

"Polly and I are sleepy, Auntie. Are we there yet?"

"Soon, sweetheart," Emma replied, remembering Michael telling her they would be on the river for four or five hours— enough to get some real sleep. Then there would be a post-chaise ride to his estate. She settled herself on the bunk, with Katie tucked beneath her arm. Doris took the opposite, narrower bunk.

There was barely enough room for the three of them, but at this point, Emma didn't care. The mattress felt good, the covers smelled clean, and they were exhausted.

In the distance, she could hear Michael and Wright, but couldn't make out what they were saying, although she thought she heard her name. Part of her wanted to listen, but she couldn't make herself move toward the voices. With fatigue quickly overtaking her, Emma tugged Katie closer. Closing her eyes, she told herself it was just for a minute.

EMMA FELT A slight nudge on her arm, drawing her back from the depths of a warm, blissful dream. A soothing sensation pulsed through her, wrapping her like a cozy blanket, and all she wanted to do was sink further into that warmth and lose herself in her dream—one filled with thoughts about *him*.

In that dream, Michael had stood before her, his luminous smile lighting up his face. His captivating green eyes twinkled with mischief, and that teasing dimple of his danced enticingly as he tugged her closer. He seemed on the verge of telling her something, yet the playful look on his face made her heart race. Was he going to kiss her?

"Emma, Katie, we're in Sussex, and the carriage is here for us."

Suddenly, her dream began to fade. It was Michael's voice, but his face had become lost in a haze. Emma didn't want to move, struggling to return to that dreamlike state, where he was going to kiss her. She moaned in protest and dug deeper into the covers, still trying to ignore reality as remnants of her dream lingered invitingly in her mind.

Michael's laughter rang out, rich and full of joy. "I see what we're about," he teased. "I'd carry you, but it might draw attention, Em, since you're dressed as a boy."

She smiled as she heard his voice, but when his words penetrated her consciousness, she bolted upright and opened her eyes. "No, you can't carry me. It wouldn't look right."

Although every part of her wanted him to.

Wilton Hall
Amberley, South Downs
Sussex, England
The next day

A THREE-STORY MANSE made of pink limestone and brick rose gently from behind a cluster of trees as the post-chaise rounded the large pond and entered the driveway. The carriage wheels crunched over oyster shells as they approached the grand Georgian house. Emma noted its unkempt appearance, with ivy covering several walls and weeds sprouting in various places along the driveway.

She wiped the last vestiges of sleep from her eyes and looked down at her niece, who lay across her lap. Doris and Katie had spent most of the long journey asleep, with Doris snoring for much of the time. Emma and Katie were still dressed as boys, believing that wearing the costumes could still help confuse anyone following them. At least there would be no staff to see her in this state of dress. But after what they had experienced with the loss of her home, the most important thing was that they had arrived without incident.

The final stretch of the trip overland was a little longer than anticipated, but not nearly as long as the one on the Thames. But it was much more comfortable. Michael had ensured they had plenty of food and drink along the way. Although she would have enjoyed it even more had he accompanied them inside the carriage instead of riding on horseback.

Wilton Hall would be her new home, at least for the time

being. Perhaps, once Evie and Martin repaired their home, they could return to being a family in London. Fleetingly, she wondered if there might be a way for them all to be together here.

Before she could fantasize any longer, the carriage halted, the door to the manse opened, and a man stepped out.

"Lady Emma Grantham, I am Lord Wilton's butler, Stanhope. Your rooms are ready for you and Miss Saunders. On behalf of the staff, welcome to Wilton Hall," he said, before suddenly sniffing and then pinching his nose to avoid a sneeze. "I apologize, my lady. I'm not used to the weather and the different smells of the country."

"Ah, Stanhope," Michael said, his boots crunching on the drive as he walked up from behind Emma. He regarded the butler with a mixture of familiarity and authority. "I trust your trip was uneventful?"

Emma would have sworn she caught a fleeting roll of the man's eyes before he replied. "Yes, my lord. We adhered to your instructions meticulously. The horses and drivers were changed at the stipulated intervals, and we drove straight through, without delay."

Michael nodded. "I understand, Stanhope. This was a special situation. Future transfers to the country will be straightforward." He paused. "And Finn… Did he make the trip without any issues?"

Stanhope opened his mouth, ready to respond, when a lively dog burst through the door, almost knocking the butler off balance. The red-and-white spaniel skidded to a stop in front of Katie, expressive eyes darting around in wonder. It tilted his head left and then right, as if taking in the curious appearance of the very little person.

Michael couldn't contain his laughter, his voice full of relief and joy. "I don't believe Finn has ever seen a child. He's excited to see someone his size."

"How is it possible that he has never encountered a child, my lord?" Emma inquired. "And I didn't realize you had a dog."

Michael flashed a brilliant smile, his dimpled gaze igniting warmth. "I found him while on an assignment. He was starved and stuck in a crate in the hull of a ship we came across. I have no idea how long he was there, but judging by the way he likes to run until he drops, I think he was rarely out of the cage."

"How awful," exclaimed Emma, her heartstrings immediately ensnared by Finn's sad story. "Of course, he would want to run."

"I had tall fences installed at this property as well as the London townhouse, so he can do so without causing anyone angst."

"Auntie, he's pretty. Can I pet him?" Katie asked, her eyes sparkling with excitement as she crouched down to get a closer look at the playful dog.

Emma glanced at Michael, who gave her an encouraging nod. "He's friendly—just energetic," he said, chuckling as the dog bounced excitedly around them. "I have a feeling he's found just the friend he needed in Katie," he added, a warm smile spreading across his face.

Giggles burst from Katie as she and Finn ran around each other on the front lawn. She was able to truly stretch her legs for the first time in two days, and Finn easily related to being pent up too long. For the first time since Emma's sister and brother-in-law had gone, things seemed *right*.

CHAPTER EIGHT

The next day

MICHAEL SIGHED, TILTING his head back slightly, allowing Hastings to get a better measure of the scruffy beard that had accumulated during his days on the road. The scraping sound of the blade against his skin was soothing, especially after his sleepless night.

"How did you sleep last night, my lord?" Hastings asked as he rinsed the blade full of whiskers mixed with frothy, sandalwood-scented soap in a bowl of warm water.

Michael grunted a reply. Hastings had an uncanny ability to read his thoughts.

"I take it you *didn't* sleep?"

"What makes you say that?"

"Well, the fact that you've been favoring your leg. You could barely bend it when you got into your bath this morning, and you winced a few minutes ago when you sat in this chair. And there's the fact that I heard you pacing back and forth most of the night."

"Next time, plug your ears with cotton."

"If you would only allow me to apply the salve that Dr. Bianchi prepared—"

"The answer is no." Michael refused to walk through his home smelling like a dead fish or dog excrement, especially around Emma.

Hastings muttered something about vanity and pride.

Yes, dammit. Michael *did* have his pride. He wasn't a dandy by any means, but he'd be damned if he'd walk around his own home smelling like a rotting animal carcass. Most of the time, he could put up with the chronic pain of his injury. It was a setback that made him hyperaware he was not invincible—something that every young man who went away to war believed in the beginning.

After witnessing the death of so many good men, so many friends in battle, he had changed. The pain in his leg was proof that he'd survived, that he was still alive to fight another day. Over time, he'd learned to push aside his physical pain. But sometimes, it became sharper and more intense. The journey from London to his estate over the past days had been designed to throw off anyone who might be following them. But it had taken a toll on his ability to ignore the pain in his leg.

Hastings gave a beleaguered sigh. "Very well, but we have received word from Dr. Bianchi that he will be in the area in the next few days. He will insist on examining your leg."

"He can insist all he wants."

"My lord, I only want to remind you that your leg can be helped."

Michael opened his eyes and saw the flash of anger on the younger man's face. Behind that anger was concern. Now it was his turn to sigh. It had been Hastings who'd dragged him from the battlefield and fought the surgeon who wanted to cut off his leg, Hastings who had nursed him through the fever and infection that followed. Hastings, who was practically a boy when he'd enlisted in the war. Hastings had saved his life. He would never question the man's loyalty.

"Very well, we'll see what Bianchi has to say when the time comes."

Hastings nodded as his deft hands smoothly slid along Michael's jaw, scraping the rough beard off. "You certainly needed a shave, my lord, even if I do say so myself. Now, please try to remain still."

Michael gave a nod and closed his eyes once more, even as his mind continued to sift through troubling details about the recent spate of arsons in London over the last several months. While only two people had died, it was clear the arsonist had intensified his heinous attacks. At first, the fires had been sporadic, but in the past month, they had become more frequent.

A sense of frustration gnawed at him as a haunting realization settled in—despite how careful they had been executing their plan to get Emma and Katie to his estate, he couldn't help but suspect that the arsonist was searching for them. He figured they were a day or two ahead of the arsonist, at best. The question was, would they be able to figure out the criminal's identity and capture him before he discovered their whereabouts?

Michael knew little for certain, but expected to receive a missive from Armstrong soon, an update on the investigation in London. But in the meantime, he would continue to prepare for all possibilities—hiring more footmen and seeing to the fortification of the crumbling stone wall that bordered the estate.

As he thought about the arsonist, he shifted restlessly in the chair.

"My lord!" Hastings pulled back, brows knitting together as whipped soap flew from his hands. "You do realize this is a *very* sharp blade? They would show me no mercy if I sliced your throat by accident. No one would believe any defense I laid out," he said in a wry tone.

Michael laughed softly and held up his hand to placate. "I apologize. You're right. It's just that when I'm supposed to stay still, my mind wanders to pressing matters. You know this about me. I'll try very hard not to move."

"Yes, but you're not usually this fidgety, and you're much more distracted than normal. Please, stay still," Hastings replied, shaking his head with both amusement and exasperation.

"You're right, once again. Several things are running through my mind, any one of which can be distracting. As a group, they are *very* distracting. Perhaps you can help me with a few things before we proceed."

"Happy to, my lord—especially if it means I won't be at risk of slicing your neck or nicking your ear. I don't like it when blood mixes in with my whipped shaving cream. Nasty business."

Michael laughed, and Hastings joined in.

"Can you find the name of the modiste in town and then invite her here to meet with Lady Grantham and Katie?" Michael asked. "Also, I need you to look into hiring more footmen to guard the perimeter. I need them more for security purposes than household chores at present. Wright plans to join us after he visits his Aunt Chippie in Brighton. With his keen instincts, he'll be an excellent asset in setting up a defense. And please handle this discreetly. I don't want to provoke Stanhope and give him the impression that I'm disregarding his household hiring authority. Of course, I will discuss it with him, but I'll tell him that Wright and I will manage it. You understand the qualities I look for in recruits for security. If you don't mind doing that, I'd appreciate it. Stanhope's expertise lies in household matters, and he will have his hands full hiring for key positions within the manor."

Hastings picked up the shaving cream. "I promise to do as you ask. Now, if you will lean back and relax, we can finish."

"Agreed. Thank you, Hastings." Michael leaned back again and tilted his head, his thoughts turning again to Katie and Emma. He realized that he was growing fonder of Katie. She was a bright child with a curious mind.

And Emma...she was another story completely, he thought, thinking of their whispered conversations on the journey while Katie and Doris had slept. His fondness had unnerved him a little, convincing him to ride his horse the last leg of the journey, while Katie, Doris, and Emma had the carriage. It had also given him a chance to keep an eye out for anyone who might have followed them, he reasoned. While they hadn't had any time since their arrival the evening before, he was very aware of her presence.

When he joined Emma and Katie in the breakfast room an hour later, Michael felt more like himself—and more certain he'd be ready, should the arsonist follow them.

As he entered the breakfast room, he found Emma and Katie discussing the food and trying to decide what would be the safest food to sneak to Finn, while the dog lay in the corner, head flat on the floor, looking in Emma and Katie's direction with doleful "feed me" eyes.

Michael couldn't help but notice how pretty Emma was—her hair was swept up in a loose chignon, and her rose-pink satin dress contrasted nicely with her red hair and violet eyes.

"Good morning, Emma and Katie…and Finn," he said, stooping to pet the dog before walking to the buffet. "Everything smells delicious," he added, picking up his plate. He noticed Katie was enjoying her toast, bacon, and eggs. Finn had settled in the corner of the room and was clearly waiting for what he hoped would be his next scrap of bacon.

"We should ask Lord Michael what Finn can eat, Katie," Emma admonished her gently.

"I would keep to the basics, Kat, and only give him things like bacon or eggs. I suppose the bananas and blueberries would be all right, but no pastries or things that are sweet," Michael said.

"That's an easy list to follow," Emma said. "Let's limit it to those few things. Will that be all right with you?"

"Yes, Auntie. I wouldn't want Finn to get a tummy ache," Katie said, kissing her aunt on the cheek. "They hurt."

"I see Finn has thrown me over for you, Katie," Michael said, ladling some eggs on his plate.

"I like Finn very much," Katie replied. "I never had a dog before, but I don't think Finn ever had a person my size before. We are the same height," she said, glancing between Michael and Finn.

Emma and Michael exchanged looks of amusement and chuckled at the precocious child.

He turned back toward the buffet table, and a smile tugged at the corners of his lips as he heard Katie speaking sweetly to Finn, and Finn softly barking in return. After enduring the harsh imprisonment and abuse in the damp, dark hull of the pirate ship, the dog had decided that spending time out of doors was not to his preference, howling each time he was placed in a pen in the stable. Originally, the stable master planned to develop a small brood of hunting dogs, making Finn the first. But it was evident that the harsh treatment of his past haunted him. A nearby neighbor had raised dogs when Michael was young, and Michael had learned a lot from him. To Michael's eye, Finn couldn't be more than two years old, given the glistening coat, the brightness of his teeth, and the abundant energy he emanated.

Had his mother been alive, she would have sent the dog to the pasture. Michael, on the other hand, had no issues with Finn living inside the house. Hastings didn't seem to care, either, yet Stanhope shot disapproving glances that pierced the air like arrows every time the dog was in his presence.

But Michael ignored that, welcoming Finn's presence in the house. He was unwilling to leave the dog in the stable, where he would howl in fear all night. He made certain the dog was kept clean with no pesky fleas and made sure he was regularly taken outside to do his necessary business.

Michael enjoyed having a loyal companion gave a sense of comfort to all their lives. In his spare time, he had trained the dog on rudimentary commands like "heel" and "sit." Still, he'd never once considered that a child was exactly what Finn needed—*until now*. Within what seemed like moments, Finn had become Katie's enthusiastic playmate. And Michael delighted seeing Katie's face as she took great pains to train Finn to play. Michael decided that, for all their sakes, he would spend some time with both and teach Katie how to walk the dog.

"My lord—" Emma began…

"Michael," he interrupted. "Please call me Michael."

She nodded and smiled sweetly. "Please forgive me…Michael."

He tried to deny it, but he loved hearing his name roll off her lips.

"I should get started getting oriented with my new duties. I'm fashioning a chatelaine to hang the keys and a few other useful household items, but I'll need the keys. I'll need to inventory the silver collection, figure out what linens we need, and there may be keys to other areas of the house, such as cupboards, that need to be collected."

"That's really not necessary," he replied, ensuring his voice remained gentle. He admired her determination, but there was no way he was actually letting her take the role of housekeeper. "I've already asked Stanhope to seek out candidates for the housekeeping position." He had no intention of having her don a chatelaine around her waist. He was grateful for an earlier discussion with Hastings, who had suggested a different approach altogether.

"Don't do that, my lord," Hastings had cautioned. "It simply won't mix well with the household. I was surprised Lady Beadle suggested it, but held my tongue. It'll confuse everyone involved. She's a lady—a woman of distinction—and to be blunt, it'll stir the servants up worse than you can imagine, having her ordering people about as the housekeeper. They won't know how to treat her, and that'll cause all sorts of chaos."

Michael had always viewed a chatelaine as more of a status symbol for a housekeeper than a useful tool—unless everything was kept under lock and key. His mother had organized their home with items stored in unlocked cabinets and did not wear any outward symbols of authority. He credited that Lady Beadle had had the best of intentions when she brought up the vacant position to Emma, her interest in securing Emma and Katie a home that would take them out of London and away from the arsonist, but he could not—no, he *would not* place a lady in that position. Emma would *not* be his housekeeper.

"I have a special request," he continued, taking on a serious tone. "But let us adjourn to the parlor down the hall."

As Michael, Emma, and Katie, with Finn in tow, left the room, they met Doris in the hallway.

"I thought Katie and Finn might enjoy going outside for a little fresh air," the maid said.

"Oh yes—Aunt Emma, may we?" Katie asked. Finn barked as if in agreement.

"Certainly. But stay close to the house," Emma said.

"We plan to stay in the gardens. They are fenced in, and I can give them some freedom without worrying about chasing after them," Doris said.

Emma laughed. "That's an excellent idea. I saw the gardens earlier this morning, and it's an excellent area for them."

The parlor wasn't nearly as nice as the breakfast room, which also needed renovation, but it provided a modicum of privacy for the impending discussion. Michael wanted to convince Emma that he needed her to help him renovate. He surveyed the room, taking in the bald spots on the carpet that had long needed replacement. The blue-and-white damask curtains hanging over the main window were soiled and frayed by dust and age.

Emma and Michael stood in the center of the room.

"As you can see, this room is in desperate need of renovation," he began. "I require someone who possesses a keen sense of interior design. I want someone who understands how furnishings work together—how colors complement each other and how they work with different spaces. I need someone with *your* skills, especially at a time when I find myself in dire need of such expertise."

"Michael, I know little about what goes into renovating a room," Emma protested, looking a little flustered.

"You understand how colors and fabrics work together, correct?" he asked.

"Well...yes. I know how a house runs, but my only experience with decorating is with my own clothing."

"You decide on fabrics you like to wear?" he persisted. "Fabrics that show your best qualities, and work well on you?"

"Well, yes. Of course. But my lo—Michael, I have never overseen decorating a room and have never decided what color paint to use on the walls."

"It's been my experience that most women have been raised to much of this. All that weighs on my mind is the expectation that, as an earl, I should possess a stylish residence and be capable of entertaining. I find myself uncertain about it, but you are used to these things. You seem well-versed in these affairs, and I suspect you have an instinct for it. Would you consider taking on that responsibility?"

Emma paused, her brows knitting together in thought. "Only on one condition, my lord—"

"Michael," he interrupted, his voice imbued with warmth.

"Yes…Michael," she continued, her tone more resolute. "I'll agree on one condition. You will be part of my selection process. That is, you tell me your favorite colors. You also must tell me what you don't like and how you want the room to feel, and…" She paused for a moment, as if to emphasize the next point. "And occasionally, accompany me to the village to give me your opinions on colors and fabrics."

"Is that truly all you need?" he asked, eyebrow raised.

She nodded firmly. "Yes, of course. Your opinion is important because this is your home, and you should enjoy your surroundings. I shan't bother you too much. I am certain you will have your hands full with the accounts and the property. Knowing what colors you like will be of great help to me. I will do my best to transform this into a place you can be proud of."

Michael's expression turned thoughtful. Lately, Michael had found himself drawn to bright reds and golds, like the colors in her hair, and the soft violet of her eyes. "There's one more item to discuss, Emma."

She looked at him with a puzzled expression. "Are you having structural changes made to the rooms?"

"No, no. Nothing like that." He cleared his throat, hoping she would accept his next suggestion. He didn't want to argue with her, but both she and Katie had meager belongings and the clothes they had managed to take with them on the night of the fire. Had they stayed with Lady Beadle, the older woman would have immediately repaired her wardrobe. "A modiste will arrive tomorrow. She will bring fashionable fabric swatches and patterns and will collaborate with you and Katie for new dresses in line with the latest fashions," Michael said, clearing his throat. He tried not to imagine Emma standing in her shift as the modiste took her measurements, but he was having a difficult time.

"No…Michael. That's too much. You've been so generous already," Emma protested.

"Nonsense." His voice was gentle, but direct. "I did not give you enough time to take care of this issue, given how quickly we left London. I insist on this and will brook no arguments. A lady needs more than one dress, and so does a little girl."

"I am not arguing. But I *insist* on paying for our clothing. I do have some funds that I was able to find before we left the house."

"No. Your money is no good here, and truly, we aren't talking about a large expense. You are doing me a big favor overseeing the refurbishment of the rooms, and you will also need suitable clothing," he said, running his hand through his hair. "I'm afraid I must insist on the wardrobe, Emma. You need clothes befitting your station."

"I understand and agree to your requests. But may I make one of my own?" she asked.

"Certainly." He wanted to make sure there would be no more discussions over what her role was in this house and was secretly thrilled she had agreed so easily to his requests.

"Stanhope pointed out the door to the attic, and I was hoping I could find time, later today, perhaps, to explore it. I would be interested in finding some of the original fabrics used in the house, and perhaps even original drawings of the house. Some of those fabrics, I think, are still hanging on windows, and I like them. I thought it might be useful, and you might favor the colors and fabrics. It would save on expenses—even though you've indicated there is plenty of money to work with, I like to economize where I can."

Michael smiled, feeling a real sense of relief. "That's a fine idea, and I agree to your request. For now, I'd like to finish walking through some of the rooms that need attention, so you can think of the order of their transition." He glanced at the clock on the mantel. "I am expecting a messenger, but should have time later today to take a look in the attic."

CHAPTER NINE

Later that afternoon

"AUNTIE, CAN FINN and me play with that stack of hats in the corner?" Katie asked, with the dog thumping his tail next to her in the attic.

"Finn and *I*," Emma said. She didn't correct her niece's grammar too often—Katie was a bright child, but sometimes in her excitement, she forgot. Emma looked at Michael, who nodded in agreement. "I think it should be fine, sweetie. Just remember to shake the dust off the hat before putting it on your head or Finn's. Dust can make you sneeze, and then you'd need another bath." She winked at her niece.

"Oh, not another bath. I'm *clean!*" Katie said.

"Well, be just as careful with Finn, or we'll have to bathe him again, too."

Finn seemed to make his objection known by getting down on his back legs and covering his eyes with his front paws, making them laugh.

"We'll be careful, won't we, Finn?" Katie looked at the dog, who gave a soft woof. "See, Auntie? He will be careful, too. I'll be extra careful to shake the hats. I'll even shake my hair after, and Finn will do the same. Right, Finn?"

Finn gave another woof.

"Well then, that should be fine," Emma said. "We'll be just over there, by the window, sorting through the trunks and the furniture."

As she and Michael made their way to the other side of the large attic, Emma looked over her shoulder and noticed that Katie was, indeed, shaking the hats. She bit her lip to keep from chuckling out loud. She didn't want to wash Katie's hair again today. Yesterday, Katie and Finn had been playing in the garden while Doris watched over them. Katie came back into the house with a head full of yellow pollen from whatever flowers she had been playing in, which required a head-to-toe bath. Even Finn required an additional cleaning.

"Why don't we start with this?" Michael suggested, opening the lid of a large, domed trunk.

"Oh my, what a treasure trove," Emma said, eyeing the many items wrapped carefully inside in thin muslin and tied with silk ribbon that had faded over time.

"I can ask one of the maids to do it for you if it's too much," Michael said.

"Don't you dare," Emma said in a mock-angry tone. "And take away my fun?" She gave him a cheeky smile.

Michael chuckled. "Well then, let's go through some of this. If we find more than a few things we can use, I'll ask several of the lads to carry everything outside so it can be properly cleaned and washed."

"Good idea. Oh my! Look at this lovely gilt-bronze mantel clock," Emma said, pulling back some tissue paper covering the clock.

"I could be mistaken, but I think that's an Ormolu clock. I recall seeing one at my grandfather's home when I was younger," Michael said.

Emma turned to him. "Do you think this could be the same clock? It was packed with special care. Do you think it could have a special meaning, perhaps a wedding present?"

"I don't know. They might have had several throughout their estates. But that's an interesting idea," Michael said as he unwrapped some matching candlesticks. "These must have been gifts—perhaps a birthday or another special occasion—to be packed so carefully."

"Those would look lovely over the mantel in the parlor," Emma said, fingering the finish on the clock. "What an amazing find." She couldn't wait to see what else the trunk held and carefully moved the clock aside before picking up another package.

This one felt light and delicate. When she finally removed the first layer of paper, she realized it was two glasses. "These could be from a very special occasion—maybe a wedding!" exclaimed Emma, delicately unwrapping the tissue from two fluted champagne glasses, engraved with Michael's family crest. "And they're signed by Baccarat."

"I'm familiar with Baccarat from my time in France. They do beautiful work, although I had no reason to purchase any," Michael said. "These probably belonged to my grandfather and grandmother. He never remarried after she died. Uncle Robert told my sister it was a love match—something rather unusual in *ton* marriages. I never gave it much thought, but perhaps this is the evidence of their love union."

Emma gazed up at him and smiled. "We may have found their silverware," she said, holding up a spoon, also with the family crest on it. "One day, I'd like to travel to France," she said longingly, re-placing the fluted glasses in the corner of the trunk. "Look. There's more." She picked up a wooden box and opened it. "This contains cutlery and silverware. I believe your grandmother may have packed this trunk. Several things in here are the types of things a mother would pass down to her daughter."

"My mother," Michael said solemnly. "She married a vicar, and my grandfather cut off communication with her. By the time he found my sister and me, Grandmama had died."

"That's so sad," Emma said, carefully closing the trunk. She turned to him. "What about that large one over there?" she asked, pointing to a brass-and-black trunk behind the one they had just investigated. He nodded, and they opened it.

Emma unwrapped a package of artfully folded tissue paper that had been meticulously arranged to protect an exquisitely folded bridal veil. "This must have belonged to the lady of the manor. It's lovely, and such an unusual thing to find. Many brides in my grandmother's and mother's days didn't wear veils on their wedding day." She held the veil up to the light, lovingly fingering the fine muslin. "Do you see the flower petals that are embroidered on it? The embroidery is so delicate and well-made."

Michael cleared his throat. "I'm unfamiliar with bridal attire, but it is a lovely veil," he said wryly.

"Nor am I," she responded. "The only wedding I ever attended was my sister's, and it was a tiny ceremony." Emma carefully re-wrapped the veil and set it aside as she combed through a box of handkerchiefs, a beautiful silver cake server, a small bundle of letters wrapped in ribbon, dried flowers, and various other items in the trunk.

"So many sweet keepsakes," she said as she closed the lid with a wistful exhale. For reasons she couldn't explain, she had hoped to find the wedding gown that went with the veil. And when she didn't, she felt disappointed about refolding the veil and tucking it back into the tissue paper, as if relegating it to a prison of timeless indifference. She had never seen anything so lovely and wondered what the dress had looked like. Perhaps it had been given to another family member who hadn't needed the veil. To her eye, the fabric showed no evidence of deterioration, thanks to the careful packing in the trunk and the lavender sachets that kept the moths away.

The only veils Emma recalled were drawings in clothing pattern books or descriptions in some of the novels she had read. Her father's older sister, Aunt Zelda, had tutted when she asked about Evie wearing one for her wedding.

"It's a lovely concept, and would look beautiful on you or Evie, but it's generally not done, Emmie. We don't want to draw negative attention to ourselves by being overly ostentatious," her aunt had told her. "I certainly didn't use one, and nor did your mother or anyone I can think of."

While she acknowledged her aunt's concerns, Emma saw the aristocracy as the epitome of extravagance, based on one of the few occasions she'd attended a ball. She also judged, given the substantial number of hats Katie had been playing with, that the former lady of the manor might have felt similarly. They were dusty and piled in the corner of the attic. Yet, she thought, the veil had been lovingly and carefully packed away. She blinked back a tear at the thought and hoped Michael had not seen it.

Beneath opulent chandeliers and polished marble floors, women of the *ton* paraded in extravagant attire. Massive hats embellished with gaudy ostrich feathers—feathers that the birds themselves would have preferred to keep—adorned their heads, bobbing into pedestrians' faces as the women sauntered through shops. And she couldn't begin to describe the fox pelts. Emma was firmly against hunting and couldn't stand looking at anyone wearing a pelt unless it was someone who genuinely needed the animal to fend off starvation to survive.

She couldn't understand the reluctance about wearing a veil, especially a veil as lovely as this one. And she couldn't help the way the veil seemed to call to her, even though she knew she would soon be considered firmly on the shelf.

"What about *that* trunk?" Emma asked, pointing to a large brown trunk against a far wall.

She watched as Michael limped over to it. "It's got a lock on it," he said. "But curiously, the key is still inserted in the lock."

She laughed. "What good is a lock if it's not locked?" Leaning back, she looked over at the far side of the attic, where Katie and Finn were merrily trying on hats, totally lost in the moment.

"Exactly," he said, pocketing the lock and key. "I don't think we should leave any locks up here that have keys with them. I don't want the curious Katie to get any ideas. She might accidentally lock herself or Finn in one of the trunks."

She glanced again at Katie and Finn, noticing that the girl was busy tying the ribbons to a bonnet on Finn's head, which made both Emma and Michael chuckle. "Oh! That would be unthinkable. You are right to be concerned. I'll be setting some rules for her regarding the attic," she said, standing and walking over to the larger trunk.

Michael took the cloth Emma had brought with her and placed it on the floor to keep her from getting dust on her clothing.

"Do you think we'll find anything useful in here?" she asked.

"I'm as curious to see as you. I didn't know this part of my family very well, and I don't recall ever meeting my grandmother or any aunts. My mother's sister, although she was considerably younger than my mother, had married and moved away by the time my sister, Lizzie, and I began to visit with my mother. And we didn't visit all that often. I barely remember what this estate looked like before I inherited the property. In any case, it was one of the minor properties—I think a summer estate, and not the main seat."

"So, was your inheritance of the title and estate a surprise?" she asked.

"Yes, it was—and there's been little explanation on my Uncle Robert's demise, except to say he had a coaching accident. From the little I had learned, he had *planned* to marry the young woman he had been betrothed to since childhood, but he had not married, and therefore, he had no heirs. The earldom held a special remainder that my mother probably didn't know about, and I only learned once the solicitors explained it to me. Special remainders are rare, but this one allowed the property to pass to me as the last male heir. My uncle was buried long before I was notified that I'd inherited an earldom."

"That must have been a daunting conversation with the late earl's solicitor," Emma remarked, pushing open the lid. Inside the trunk, she discovered exactly what she was looking for. "Look, Michael! There are bolts of fabric, all wrapped in tissue paper. And here are drawings of rooms, even with the placement of furnishings. And here—"

"Are drawings of the grounds, when they were in their heyday," he said, unrolling a scrolled bundle of parchment she'd handed him. "This is excellent. It shows the rock wall when it was first built. This will certainly help in my quest to rebuild the damaged areas. And this section looks like a plan for large stables. The existing stables are much smaller than what is depicted in this drawing."

Emma noticed something shining wedged between two packages. She reached for and pulled out a small brass-and-wood-handled penknife, just like the one she had often seen Martin use to open packages delivered to the house. *Michael might appreciate that for his desk,* she thought. *Maybe I can find a way to clean it up for him.* Glancing in his direction, she noticed he seemed to be still absorbed in the drawings of the property, so she tucked the penknife into her pocket, planning to clean it properly later.

She looked at him as he stood next to her, combing through the packages of fabrics and the scrolls of drawings. It made her feel warm all over when he was near—something she'd only begun to experience after she met him and found herself in his company.

Hoping to distract herself, she examined a bolt of blue damask. "Do you favor blue? I imagine this cloth was intended for covering chairs." She looked around and spotted some chairs in the corner, covered with cloth to shield them from the dust.

"I rather like the color. It's calming. I could easily be happy with blues throughout the manse," he said, leaning down closer and bringing his face next to hers.

She was very aware of his presence, as a blush heated her face. With his face this close to hers, she wondered what it would be like if he kissed her. She gave herself a mental shake and blurted, "My room at Evie's was in blues and white. I loved the colors. And you're right, they did feel calming."

As he helped her up, she tripped on the cloth on the floor. When he caught her by the waist, they stood mere inches apart.

"Eek! A bat!" Katie's scream sliced through the stillness of the room, shattering the fragile moment. It was followed by a loud yip and a crash, with the chaotic sound of her tiny feet mingled with those of the dog in full gallop racing in their direction. "Aunt Emma, where are you?" Katie cried out, her voice filled with panic.

"I'm right here, darling," Emma said, her voice strained.

"Are you all right?" Michael asked. "Your face has gone ashen."

"I'm quite terrified of bats," she admitted, clutching the damask she had been examining while scanning the ceiling.

"They won't bother you," Michael said. "But I don't want to think of them occupying the attic. I'll send some footmen to come up here and catch them; they can release them far from the house. Otherwise, we'll have an abundance of bat droppings to contend with, and it could ruin the furnishings."

CHAPTER TEN

Late that night

MICHAEL LAY IN bed, twisting beneath the damp sheets, his mind a whirlwind of the day's events. When he closed his eyes, his memory of his visit to the attic flooded back, vivid and haunting, making it impossible to sleep. An image of Emma wearing the bridal veil she had looked so longingly at took shape and played over and over in his head. She was running through a meadow...but he couldn't see the person she was running toward. It was an unyielding loop, intensifying the frustration that had plagued him all day. In the recesses of his mind, he could hear deep male laughter echoing, taunting him with a familiarity, yet never revealing a face. A mysterious figure just out of his reach.

He wasn't ready for marriage, but the thought of her wedding someone else sent a wave of nausea and despair through him.

Finally, overwhelmed by the incessant replaying of feelings and unable to allow the torture to continue, Michael opened his eyes.

His leg ached so badly that sweat beaded on his forehead. Luckily, he wasn't keeping Finn awake with his tossing and turning. The dog had been sleeping next to Katie, which pleased Michael immensely. The child had experienced several night-mares since they arrived, and having Finn sleep next to her had quelled the bad dreams right away. On the first night they were there, the child had awakened the household with a bloodcurdling scream. Michael rushed to Katie's room, with Finn on his heels. The dog had licked Katie's face, calming her. Emma joined him and they had both stayed with the child as she calmed down. When it was clear Katie had fallen asleep, Emma suggested he take Finn back to his room, but he pointed to the bed. Both Katie and Finn had fallen asleep, a tangle of paws and arms, with gentle snores coming from both. Finn was where he needed to be.

Emma had gazed up at him with those luminous violet eyes—it was all he could do to keep from sweeping her into his arms and kissing her. He'd had the same reaction when they were in the attic searching through trunks, and she held up that veil. An image flashed through his mind of Emma dressed in a wedding gown, the delicate veil over her luscious red hair. Later, she tripped on the cloth she'd been kneeling on while going through the trunks, and he'd caught her around the waist and once again had the urge to kiss those plump pink lips.

Katie's scream had snapped him from that. It had been complete chaos after she and Finn discovered a bat. It turned out to be a single baby bat that had slipped in through a small hole in a broken attic window. The ruined window and the bat might have gone unnoticed if not for the day's events, Michael thought sardonically. Stanhope had sent two footmen to the attic, but they found no other bats. The only droppings they found could be attributed to the baby, which they captured and released. They watched the bat fly toward an old building behind the stables. Michael reasoned that it had family in that old building and knew its way home.

He needed to be more careful around Emma. She was not his to kiss. His role was to protect both her and Katie, keeping them safe while Armstrong and his friends worked behind the scenes to track down the arsonist. Michael wished he could be out there looking for the bastard as well, but watching over Emma and Katie was more important, and he would guard them with his very life.

After spending hours wrestling with the pain, Michael heaved a heavy sigh, knowing he wouldn't get any sleep, and sat up, swinging his legs over the side of the bed. Frustrated, he got up and decided to go to his study to have a glass of brandy or find a book to read—anything to get his mind off picturing Emma in ways that he shouldn't. Perhaps he could spend more time on the scrolls they had found in the attic. He'd left them on his study desk. The original plans for the wall were a perfect resource to use in fixing it. So, he stood, pulled on his banyan, and lit a candle.

As he rounded the stairwell to the first floor, he saw a light shining beneath his study door. Earlier in the day, he had placed the colorfully spined gothic novels Emma had found in a trunk on one of the shelves. He planned to show her on the morrow.

As Michael approached the study, he heard a scraping noise. He paused and listened at the door. Hearing nothing else, he opened the door and saw Emma standing at the top of the ladder. Moonlight streamed in from the window behind his desk, casting a soft glow around her, allowing him to see the slender curves of her figure through the silky, translucent robe. She was obviously unaware of the sight she created for him. He almost groaned aloud.

"What the hell are you doing up there, Emma? You'll fall," he said gruffly, far gruffer than he'd intended. But hell, she was the one standing up on a ladder looking like a siren.

She gasped and twisted around on the ladder toward him. "Oh!" she exclaimed as she lost her footing and fell, a scream catching in her throat—only, her fall was broken by soft arms and a hard chest.

Emma was slender and petite, but the momentum of catching her mid-fall from the ladder, combined with the strain on his stiffened leg, threw him off balance. He stumbled backward, and before he could right himself, they were both going down. Twisting instinctively, he turned to shield her, absorbing the brunt of the impact with his wounded leg.

"Michael! Are you all right?" she cried.

He grunted and slowly opened his eyes. Even through the haze of pain, all he could see was her. With such proximity, he could smell her—a gentle jasmine scent that wafted around her as she straddled his chest, looking down at him with those gorgeous violet eyes.

"Your eyes look like a midnight sky, and you smell like heaven," he rasped, and then he tightened his arms around her and finally gave in to what he'd been wanting to do since the moment he'd met her.

"Emma?" he asked, pulling away and seeing her shocked expression. "Are you all right?"

"I am," she replied, staring down at him, a smile lifting the corner of her mouth. "You kissed me."

He chuckled. "Yes, yes, I did. And I would love to do it again—with your permission, of course."

She shifted, and he groaned.

"Oh, Michael. Your leg!" she exclaimed, scrambling off him. "I've hurt it. Let me help you up." She reached for him and was trying to pull him to his feet when a male voice sounded from behind her.

"My lady, my lord, what happened here?" Hastings asked. "My lord, are you injured?"

Michael refused to acknowledge pain in front of Emma. "Truly, Hastings, I'm fine. I suffered a slight mishap, is all. And Lady Emma arrived to help. I had trouble sleeping and decided to look for a book." He nodded to the ladder. "I reached for a book and my foot slipped on the step, causing me to slip. Emma had been in the kitchen and heard my fall and came to help."

Hastings looked from one to the other. It was obvious to Michael that the man didn't believe the story. Nevertheless, he knew Hastings would keep his thoughts to himself. The valet leaned down and helped him up. "I should take him to his room and take care of this leg, my lady," he said.

Together, Hastings and Emma helped Michael up and walked

him back upstairs to his room. As they stood there, Emma asked, "Do you need anything else?"

"I don't think so," he replied, his voice thick with reluctance, each word heavy on his tongue. The truth was that he was mentally preparing to walk away from the warmth of her presence. He stifled a grimace, fighting against the sharp twinge of pain in his leg that mingled with the frustration of not being able to kiss her once more. Hastings would see to his leg, he reassured himself, but for the moment, all he could focus on was her.

She gently brushed her fingers across her lips and looked up at him with wide, innocent eyes. The lingering memory of their passionate kisses in those few, too-brief moments they had been alone felt like a sweet ache he couldn't reach, nearly pushing him to the brink of vexation. Her lips were still swollen from their kisses only minutes earlier, and her beautiful violet eyes held the same innocent look they had when she'd landed on top of him.

"Goodnight, Emma." His words felt forced, even to him. It was impossibly unfair to have been so close to the object of his longing and desire.

"Goodnight, Michael," she replied, two fingers to her swollen lips.

As Hastings closed the door, Michael stared at it, loathing the thick, carved wood that separated him from Emma. He knew there would be no sleep for the rest of the night, and it wouldn't have anything to do with the pain in his leg.

CHAPTER ELEVEN

The next morning

My God! He kissed me. And I loved it.

Emma lay in her bed, staring up at the ceiling, exhaustion demanding that she stay there and force herself to sleep longer. She let out a long sigh. "It won't matter how long I stay in bed," she admitted a little above a whisper. "I know I won't sleep another wink."

So much had happened the day before that when she closed her eyes, memories of the day and night spiraled vividly through her mind. Just the thought of Michael's smoldering kiss sent waves of pleasure rippling through her body. Closing her eyes, she replayed the scene in her mind—how he had caught her as she fell to the floor of his library and then kissed her. While her lips tingled from the memory of his touch, it was her heart that couldn't let go.

What would have happened if Hastings hadn't shown up? A wave of excitement shot through her as she recalled the sense of frustration over being separated from Michael.

He'd kept his promise to her, and they'd spent an entire day in the attic, combing through the trunks and attic space looking for things that Emma could use in redecorating. He was the easiest man to be around, Emma decided. Despite a sometimes-gruff demeanor, she found Michael a caring, honorable man—a man she was realizing more and more that she wanted to be around.

There had been so much to look at, but it was the beautiful veil that stole her attention. While nothing identified exactly who it had belonged to, Emma had the feeling it had been Michael's grandmother's. It was the loveliest bridal creation she could remember seeing. Fitful dreams of it had driven her from her bed after hours of trying to sleep. In her dream, she ran and laughed, wearing the veil that flowed beautifully behind her as she dashed through a flower-filled meadow.

Was it *her* wedding she kept dreaming of? No matter how hard she tried, Emma couldn't make sense of the dreams. Each time she closed her eyes, the dream repeated itself. And each time she revisited the dream, she struggled to see the dress that matched her veil, only to end up disappointed. To make matters worse, she heard deep male laughter in the background, but she couldn't recognize who it was.

Her obsessive thoughts of that veil, coupled with her exhaustion from the day's events, should have been enough to lull her to sleep. But her tingling lips kept her awake. *Michael kissed me,* her heart sang over and over. No matter her other thoughts, this was the one she clung to.

She heard voices in the hall and the bark of a dog. "I should get up," she murmured. "I cannot lie here and dream of yesterday and waste the day before me. And if I don't get out of bed, the two of them will bound in here and take over my bed." Sitting up, she swung her feet over the side of the bed into the worn slippers, an act that reminded her of a few hours ago, when she had gone to the study for a book to help her sleep.

A knock sounded on her door, and she reached for her wrapper as Doris entered the room with Katie at her side.

"My lady, you've received a letter," the maid said, handing the correspondence to Emma. "Stanhope asked that I bring it to you immediately. I should return downstairs to watch for the modiste."

Emma gave a quick nod, and the maid left the room, leaving her alone with Katie and the dog.

"My sister!" she said, clasping the letter to her chest. A tremor of excitement rushed through her. She had missed her sister so much. Emma patted the bed next to her, signaling for Katie to climb up. Once the girl snuggled beneath Emma's arm, Finn jumped onto the bed and tucked himself against Katie, as Emma broke the seal on the letter.

"I miss my mama and daddy, Auntie," Katie said, a hint of sorrow in her voice.

"It appears Finn is trying to comfort you, Katie," Emma said tenderly, unfolding the letter.

"He's my best friend, Auntie. I can't wait for him to meet Mummy and Daddy," Katie said, hugging Finn tight.

"Let's see what Mummy has to say, little one," Emma said, feeling a tear slide down her cheek.

Dearest Emma and Katie,

Martin and I heard the horrible news about our home. Please don't worry about anything, Emma, and no servant was injured. We know you are prone to worry, but the most important thing is that the two of you are safe. As I understand it, you are both in Sussex, staying at Lord Wilton's manor house. Lord Wilton is an honorable man and will keep the two of you safe until we can join you.

We would come immediately, but the most important thing for us to do is find another home for all of us. It may be a few more weeks before we can be there. Martin's parents have asked that we stay, and since things have gone better than usual, we have indeed agreed to stay for a little while. We miss you both terribly.

We are working to return as quickly as possible, but we must stay here until we can secure new housing. As soon as we know, we will come and get you both.

We can replace the belongings, but not those precious to us. Thank you for taking such good care of Katie. And thank you, Emma, for saving our horses. Lord Armstrong wrote and said that you rode them to safety, and he has transferred them to his estate for the time being. I know they are horses, but they are special to us and feel like family.

We love you both and miss you both. Katie, please do as Auntie Emma tells you to do. I miss you so much. Mummy and Daddy will be there to get you before you know it!

Much love,
Evie and Martin
(Mummy and Daddy)

After reading the letter to Katie, Emma wiped another tear from the corner of her eye and noticed that the child did the same. Finn jumped up on Katie's lap and licked her face.

"We are safe," Emma said. "And we are happy." She looked at her niece. "You seem very happy. Are you?"

"Yes, very. We've had quite the adventure," Katie said enthusiastically. "But I miss Mummy and Daddy."

"Of course—we *both* miss them. This is a good time to remind you that you and Finn should stay close to the manor house, and have either me or Doris, or even Lord Michael, outside with you. Do not go anywhere without letting me know first," Emma emphasized. And as much as she hated to add the next, she did. "And if you see that man from the day of the fire, please don't go near him. Let me know as soon as possible." As safe as they were, Emma couldn't dismiss a nagging thought that she needed to stay very aware of her surroundings. Surely it had nothing to do with Michael, who considered it his mission to keep them safe—even though things had heated up considerably when she was alone in his presence. Until the arsonist was caught, she imagined she'd worry.

"Woof!" Finn said, as if to reply, *it'll be all right, Katie.*

"You'd like my mummy and daddy, Finn. They give the best goodnight kisses and hugs..." Katie started.

"Miss Katie, Lady Emma," Doris said, returning, "the modiste has arrived."

Later that morning

THE MODISTE, THE esteemed Madame Darnelle, entered with an air of elegance, accompanied by two assistants carrying overflowing boxes and bolts of fabric. Their arrival filled the room with an energy Emma wasn't sure she was ready to face. She still felt awkward having all her clothing, including her delicate garments, replaced by a man she had encountered less than a week ago, and a wave of anxiety coursed through her. Trying to steady her frazzled nerves, she took a sip of Mrs. Peppers's soothing mint tea, letting the warm liquid calm her troubled mind as she reminded herself to breathe.

Stanhope had prepared one of the larger bedroom suites for the modiste to use, giving both Katie and Emma, as well as Finn, who hadn't left Katie's side these past few days, lots of room to work with the dressmaker. Mrs. Peppers had arranged for a carafe of mint tea, a pitcher of lemonade for Katie and the assistants, and finger sandwiches and other tempting treats. She had even provided a meaty bone and a small plate of treats to keep Finn occupied.

"Lady Emma, I am so happy with the canvas I have to work with. May I say that your figure is perfection?" Madame Darnelle gushed, whirling about Emma's body with a measuring tape, then calling out measurements to one of her assistants.

The other assistant had Katie standing on a footstool, measuring her for several day dresses. There was also a box of shoes for them to choose from. Surprisingly, the shoes and slippers fit both Emma and Katie perfectly—puzzling, to be sure. Had Michael snuck into their bedchambers and measured their shoes while they were asleep? How else would he have known what sizes to give the modiste?

Impossible. He would have sent one of the maids to do it, she decided. That must have been how he did it. Still, his thoughtfulness brought a lump to her throat.

Michael was truly a kind man, even if he pretended to be grumpy, she thought with a private smile. She became even more determined to do everything she could in the time they were here to make over the parlor and any other room that Michael wanted to refurbish. They were off to a good start after they visited the attic. She'd discovered several beautiful pieces of furniture and decorative items that would add warmth to the parlor and make it a welcoming room.

The modiste's exclamation of delight brought Emma out of her musings and focused her attention once more on the fitting.

"This deep gold color brings out the violet in your eyes, Lady Emma," Madame Darnelle enthused. "Not every woman can wear this particular shade of dark, golden yellow, my lady; on some women this shade looks like mustard and makes their complexion appear sallow, but those women do not have your coloring. The richness of your red hair, your alabaster skin, and your violet eyes are *magnifique* and most unusual."

The modiste's effusive praise caused Emma's face to flush. No one had ever given her so many compliments on her appearance—except her sister Evie, who constantly reminded her how much she resembled their beautiful mother. Mama had passed away so early in their lives that Evie had been both sister and mother to Emma.

"Would we be able to stop for a few minutes? I'd love to have a cup of tea," Emma said an hour later. She had been standing on a stool, holding her arms out, for almost the entire time, and suddenly felt the need for more soothing mint tea.

"Of course!" Madame Darnelle replied. "It will give me time to show you some of my readymade garments we just finished, which I correctly guessed would be perfect on you and your niece. We can make any adjustments while we are here."

Emma nodded with a smile as she stepped down from the stool.

"Look, Auntie Emma! Finn is standing too," Katie said as she hopped down from her stool. "He's ready for his measurements to be taken. I think he'd like one of those vests that Lord Michael wears." She giggled and clapped as Finn stood up on his hind legs and hopped in a circle.

"I think he is ready for the circus," Emma said from the table where she was pouring tea for everyone, pleased that Mrs. Peppers had prepared such an abundant feast.

"*Mon Dieu*, I have never seen a dog with such talent," Madame Darnelle said with amusement.

"Madame, Finn has red hair just like Auntie. Would that mustard-colored material look good on him, too?" Katie asked.

The modiste laughed, and her assistants chuckled along with Emma. "What a charming child you are, *chérie*," she said, crouching beside Katie to tuck a brown curl behind her ear. "I think perhaps we can make him a vest and a very jaunty neckerchief as well. I believe Finn will look quite smart. What do you think?"

"Oh, I think that would be splendid!" Katie cried, clapping her hands again. "Auntie, can Finn have a bandana?"

"Of course, sweetie—if Madame Darnelle has time to make one."

"Oh, it will be no problem," the modiste said with a snap of her fingers. "We shall make him several—one to match each of your new dresses, *chérie*. He will look very dapper. *Oui?*"

"*Oui!*" Katie shouted, bouncing up and down. Finn gave a soft woof and wagged his tail in approval, sending them all into laughter once again. "Do you like the pink dress on me, Auntie? Pink is my favorite color, you know," she said, taking a bite of a biscuit before passing it to Finn to finish.

"Katie," Emma said gently, "remember what Lord Michael said about overfeeding Finn. If we give him sugary things, it might make him sick."

"I'm sorry, Auntie. I forgot."

"Well then, it's good that Mrs. Peppers sent along a small tray for him," Emma said, smiling at her niece. "I think Finn will approve." She lifted the silver dome off the plate, revealing a couple of strips of bacon along with a small bowl of blueberries and strawberries—foods that Michael had approved for Finn's snacking.

Katie beamed. "You cannot have any more of my biscuit, Finn. But if you behave, I shall give you a piece of bacon."

"As long as you wash your hands afterward," Emma reminded her, nodding at the pitcher of water and bowl in the corner of the room. She was confident Katie would obey.

The sight of the colorful fabrics and the sound of the modiste's cheerful chatter stirred something deep in Emma—echoes of long-ago afternoons spent with her mother and sister in colorful, bustling boutiques tucked along London streets, where bolts of ribbon and spools of lace had once seemed like treasures waiting to be discovered.

She had been so young then. The memories were soft around the edges, more feeling than fact—her mother's bright smile, the rustle of silk, the way her laughter had made even the plainest day feel like a celebration. Evie remembered so much more. Her older sister could recount entire scenes: what their mother wore, what they'd chosen, what they'd eaten afterward. Over the years, Evie had gently filled in Emma's faded recollections, like mending a tapestry worn thin.

But now, in this unfamiliar place, those memories brought more ache than comfort.

Emma's gaze shifted to Katie, who was twirling in delight, utterly captivated by the idea of dressing Finn in a neckerchief to match her dress. That sweet, uncomplicated joy tugged at Emma's heart. She was grateful for it, grateful for the safety the estate provided, for the kindness shown to them here.

And yet beneath that gratitude pulsed something restless and uncertain.

She didn't know how long they would need to stay. The arsonist was still out there. The smoldering remains of their home were a reminder that the world could turn on its axis in a single night. Though the manor was peaceful and the people generous, Emma couldn't shake the feeling that her life—and Katie's—was suspended in midair, like a breath waiting to be released. The weight of responsibility settled on her shoulders; she had a huge task of outfitting the manor house—something very important to Michael—and her conscience would not allow her to leave until the job was finished.

Would things ever be normal again?

She wasn't sure she remembered what *normal* felt like.

"My lady, how do you feel about this bronze silk?" the modiste asked, holding up a bolt of the shimmering silk.

"It's the most beautiful fabric I've ever seen," Emma said with a little awe as she smoothed her fingers over the rich material. "Perhaps it's too luxurious for a day dress?"

"*Non*, this is not for a day dress, my lady," the modiste said with a smile. "Lord Wilton requested at least one formal gown for you."

Emma suppressed a sigh of frustration. She'd accepted the fact that she needed a few simple dresses for every day and shifts and a pair of shoes…but a ball gown? Michael was being far too generous. But she would not say anything in front of the modiste—it would be an insult to Michael. Instead, she smiled and said, "I love it. Do you have a style in mind?"

"I do," Madame Darnelle enthused. "If you will trust me to complete it, I would like to surprise you."

Emma nodded, her mind whirling at all the beautiful fabrics and undergarments surrounding her. She was grateful for Michael's generosity but had no idea where she would wear most of these clothes. Thus far, she had selected a deep mauve velvet for a riding habit along with various fabrics in sapphire blue, deep gold, and rich amethyst. In addition, the skilled modiste had seen to every detail, ensuring all the necessary undergarments, pelisses, shoes, fashionable hats, and soft gloves were chosen. Among the readymade items, Emma had selected an emerald-green dress and a dusty-rose gown with a fresh floral pattern, along with a lovely traveling dress in a darker damask blue. She marveled that she'd never owned so many items of clothing before.

Nearby, Katie brimmed with enthusiasm. She'd wanted to choose every fabric she saw, but Emma gently reminded her that for now, selecting five would be more than enough. Katie beamed as she'd chosen several readymade day dresses, including one in the same dusty-pink fabric as Emma's, along with warm nightgowns and several dresses she could wear when playing outside that were of sturdier material, as well as the pretty shoes and charming ribbons in myriad colors, and a traveling cloak that would keep her warm—everything a young girl could desire.

The modiste approached her and Katie as they were looking through the pretty hair ribbons.

"My lady, Franchette and Aimee have already finished the alterations to the readymade gowns for both you and Miss Katie." She and her assistants helped Katie and Emma into the matching dusty-rose gowns. "Oh, you are both a picture of youthful beauty!" she exclaimed. They had even fashioned a neckerchief for Finn from a bright blue scrap and now tied it around his neck.

"We shall return in two days with the rest of the garments for a final fitting," Madame Darnelle proclaimed at last.

Emma was astonished. "I'm certain that with your full roster of clients, you already have so much on your plate. Please take your time—I do not want to add to your workload."

"The earl is an important man. Do not worry, Lady Emma. I have many seamstresses working for me, and I have hired several more. It is good to be busy, *n'est-ce-pas?*" The modiste smiled at her assistants, who both nodded enthusiastically. "It is because of such generous patrons as Lord Wilton that my establishment is thriving and that I can provide employment to good women who are talented with needle and thread. We are a busy hive of bees, and we enjoy our work," she continued, smiling. "It has been a pleasure meeting you, Lady Emma, and your darling niece, Miss Katie, and of course Master Finn, who has kept us so entertained with his many, clever tricks." Turning to Katie, she added, "And we will remember the waistcoat and other neckerchiefs for Master Finn."

Katie yet again clapped with delight. "Do you hear that, Finn? You'll be the finest-dressed dog in the district!" Finn stood on his hind legs and turned in a circle—a favorite trick.

"That is most kind of you. Thank you," Emma said, as she began to neatly fold the handkerchiefs that the modiste had thoughtfully provided.

"*Non, non, non,* my lady. We will fold and press everything and have it placed in your bedchamber and in Miss Katie's room. Mr. Stanhope has already planned for two of the maids to assist." As Madame Darnelle spoke, a soft knock sounded on the door, and two of the younger maids, Mary and Ellen, entered. They smiled and curtsied as the modiste began to direct them on where to take things.

Impulsively, Emma embraced the older woman and thanked her again.

The modiste blinked back tears and kissed Katie on both cheeks—"As they do in France," she said—and gave Finn a pat on the head. "It has been a pleasure and a joy to work with you ladies. And you, too, Finn."

"Well, I think perhaps we should take Finn for his walk," Emma said. "Thank you again, Madame Darnelle." She took Katie's hand, and they left the modiste and the women to finish up. Madame Darnelle's kindness and warmth had made Emma's anxiety fade away. And she was feeling as excited as Katie about the dresses.

As they made their way downstairs and outside to the garden, she wondered what Michael would think about the new gowns. She realized that she wanted him to like the dresses. She wanted him to notice her.

And that realization made everything just a bit more complicated.

25 Curzon Street
Mayfair, London, England
That evening

FROM THE SHADOWS across the street, Morgrave stared at the townhouse at 25 Curzon. The interfering old woman deserved what was coming. His jaw was clenched. His hands opened and closed in agitation. The sky was a deep shade of violet, the shade that made a fire seem holy. It had been days since he'd last seen her, and more since he'd experienced the wonder of the flames. Simms had chased the carriage believed to be carrying both her and the girl for hours, eventually losing the vehicle in a throng of black conveyances on the turnpike that bore a resemblance. But Morgrave hadn't given up. He wouldn't.

He could have sworn he had her pinned early on at that post-ing inn, but when he finally convinced a maid to let him check, he'd found no trace of her. *She had disappeared, but to where?*

His first sight of her was burned in his memory. As flames engulfed the home she'd lived in, slowly reducing it to smolder-ing ash, she'd paused on her horse and turned back. Not just to look at the house, but to seek him out...*him*. The fire's glow flickered in her eyes as she looked at him. He'd never allowed anyone to look upon him, always hiding his face when he lit the fires. That made her dangerous; that made her different from the others. But the combination of fear and horror in her expression, mirrored in the dance of the flames, excited him. When he found her, he would make her repeat it—and he would relish every moment.

Morgrave stood in the shadows, a sinister smile creeping across his face as he watched the lights being snuffed out inside the house across the street. The activity moved from one end of the building to the other as the occupants prepared for bed. He had been given a sign, one that affirmed his belief that the fires would purge London of the evil that had robbed him of his rightful life. More than a mere sign, the woman was fire come to life, and he would have her. After all, fire—*she*—had always been part of him, and it was right that they should be together now.

From his earliest memories, fire had been his sanctuary. She had been the one entity that gave him power, made him feel his full strength, feel the inherent power he would wield. Fire made him invincible. And now, his flame had made herself into a woman—*his* woman. Possessing her was not merely a desire; it was his fate. She was as vital as the air he breathed.

Lady Beadle knew her whereabouts—of that, he was certain—and the interfering old woman would tell him. He'd make certain. His mind whirled with ideas and schemes, calculating exactly how he would make her reveal the truth. Quickly, he settled his plan. It required daring, precision, and control—everything he excelled at. He planned to watch every movement. Like always.

Yes, the hunt has just begun...

CHAPTER TWELVE

Two days later

"AS RUNDOWN AS I found this manor house, I was surprised to discover that there was a well-maintained game room, of all things," Michael said before taking a swig of his brandy. "The rest of the house was allowed to go to hell in a handbasket, but the billiard room was maintained as if it were part of White's," he added. "How would you feel about a game of billiards?"

"I'd feel right at home," Wright said, nursing his own brandy. "It seems this room was also maintained well." He nodded to the burgundy leather seats they sat in, and the matching leather couch across the room, near a wall filled with bookshelves.

"Good. By the way, how did your visit with Aunt Chippie go?" Michael asked, topping up both of their glasses. "I thought you might be detained longer, but I am pleased you were able to rejoin us so quickly."

"She's as hale and hearty as ever." Wright chuckled. "She gets out of sorts if I don't stop by for a visit when I'm in the area. She's quite the character. My family and I visited her nearly every summer, growing up. Of course, Gran and my sisters are going to spend the summer with her. I'll be escorting them next month. And I'll have to put up with both Gran and Aunt Chippie conspiring to marry me off. Like that will happen anytime soon."

Michael arched an eyebrow. "Given how much you enjoy the

company of the widow Fulbright—and I also heard there was an actress or an opera singer somewhere waiting in the wings—I believe you."

"Damn Armstrong for his wagging tongue. He's a worse gossip than Aunt Chippie."

Michael threw back his head and laughed.

"I'm quite happy with my bachelorhood," Wright said, sounding reflective. "Besides, it seems there are fewer and fewer of us left. Although I suppose it wouldn't be out of the question if one were to meet the caliber of woman that Armstrong did. Even your sister was snapped up by in." He chuckled again.

"Hmm… Too true," Michael said, swirling his brandy. "Lizzie and Sin are ridiculously happy with their growing family." When he had inherited his title along with the various properties under his helm, it was all he could do to focus his time and energy on bringing them all up to snuff. Attending Society balls and making himself a prime target for matchmaking mamas was the last thing he wanted to subject himself to.

"Speaking of those ridiculously content married men, have you heard from Armstrong?" Wright asked.

"I haven't received a missive yet. Then again, we arrived less than a week ago. I had hoped to receive an update on the situation in London regarding the arsonist. If I haven't heard from Armstrong by tomorrow, I'll send a messenger to London. In the meantime, we have plenty to do here. I'd appreciate your help securing and fortifying the property. I've already spoken to Hastings about hiring more footmen to guard the perimeter, but I also need to reinforce the walls. There are at least a dozen spots where it has crumbled. To be honest, I wanted to add a few extra feet to its height. Conveniently, I've stumbled upon the original plans, so it should make things easier."

"I'm happy to help with that. We can inquire in the village about local tradesmen," Wright said.

"I agree. Hastings has informed me there are plenty of talented stonemasons in the area."

"Ah, that reminds me!" Wright exclaimed. "Aunt Chippie was showing me her latest portrait, and I've never seen anything more lifelike. The artist, Mr. Craig Burns, is quite a talent. He's become a personal friend of hers and has created several paintings for her. He's the newest social obsession in Brighton!"

Michael laughed. "You're jesting. Your aunt is promoting a portrait artist?"

"I'm serious. I counted five new portraits of her hanging in her townhouse."

"Your aunt is a true original," Michael said.

"She is, indeed. However, it was the sketches Mr. Burns made that captured my attention. I think he can supply an important link to the arsonist. These were not only sketches of Aunt Chippie—they also included depictions of her previous pets, as well as her parents and siblings when they were younger. I was struck by the lifelike appearance and the detail of the drawings. I told Aunt Chippie about what Lady Emma and Katie had been through, and she suggested that perhaps Mr. Burns could help. I met with him, and I must admit he's brilliant at his craft. I hope you don't mind, but I invited him here."

"That's a capital idea," Michael said. "It could give us the break we've been looking for in finding this arsonist."

"I thought you'd agree," Wright replied. "Burns can transform the verbal descriptions provided by Katie and Lady Emma into a depiction of the face of the arsonist. I've also sent a missive to Headquarters, suggesting they meet with him. He's more skilled than any sketch artist I've worked with on Crown business and could be invaluable in pursuing criminals."

"No question! Thank you for inviting him. Knowing what the arsonist looks like will give us better protection," Michael said. "Given that I'm hiring additional men to guard the property, they will be much more effective with a good description of the villain. Not to mention, we can send a copy to Armstrong, who has more contacts in London than anyone I know. I'd like to get this resolved—it's stressful for everyone, especially Emma and Katie."

"You're on a first-name basis?" Wright teased good-naturedly.

"It became easier. We've spent a lot of time in each other's company," Michael said, finding himself irritated by his friend's comment.

"Fair enough," Wright said with a smile. "Do you think Lady Emma and Katie will be able to recall the arsonist?"

"Well, Katie got a better look at him," Michael said. "But I've been reluctant to ask her, given the trauma she's been through. She was having bad dreams, but Finn helped with that. He's become her champion and sleeps at the foot of her bed now."

"That dog is an old soul."

"He certainly is."

The sounds of a bark and sweet, feminine giggles from the garden wafted in through the open window, carried by the warm breeze. Michael turned, his gaze drawn to the scene outside, where Emma and Katie watched the playful spaniel standing on his hind legs, clearly attempting some trick. Their joy was infectious, even from a distance. Emma looked lovely in a dark-pink dress, especially with her red hair shimmering in the sunshine. As he studied the scene below, his thoughts returned to the feel of her warm lips on his in the library of her hands in his hair at the nape of his neck. Giving his head a slight shake, he tried harder to stay in the moment but could not turn away. His chest tightened at the sight of Emma's smile, aimed affectionately at Katie and Finn—a smile that he yearned to have directed at him.

"And other than the bad dreams, how are Katie and Lady Emma doing?" Wright said, nodding at the window and forcing Michael from his reverie.

"They are both doing well under the circumstances," Michael replied, shooting him a narrow-eyed look. Wright was a good man and a dear friend, but he was also a rogue through and through. Women seemed to fall at his feet. Michael would make sure Emma wasn't one of them.

"Easy, man, cool your heels. I was merely inquiring how she

is settling in here." Wright flashed a grin. "No need to act the jealous suitor." He lifted his glass as though in a salute and took a sip.

"She's settling in fine," Michael mumbled. "And I am not acting in any way, least of all as a suitor. Lady Emma and her niece are under my protection. That's all. There's a madman on the loose, or have you forgotten?"

"I haven't forgotten," Wright said, setting his glass down on the side table. "But I also have eyes, and I saw the tender way Lady Emma looked at you when we were on the boat. And the attentive way you responded."

"Well, let me be clear. I am looking out for her welfare. That is all that you saw, and only that."

Wright held up his hands in surrender, but his eyes held a teasing glint. "Of course. If you say so."

"I *do* say so. And don't go getting any notions about her either."

"I promise to be on my best behavior when in her company," Wright said with a grin.

"Good. Glad we cleared that up."

"Now, how about you show me this game room that you were bragging about?"

Michael nodded and led the way. The gaming room was connected to the study and did not have a direct entrance from the hallway; one gained entry from a wood panel in the study that you tapped on the upper-right side of the panel, triggering a hinge that made it slide open. "I didn't notice this at first. It was Finn who saw it, sniffing at the wood paneling, scratching and whimpering until I investigated," he said.

Wright whistled in appreciation as they stepped into the room.

"My Uncle Robert, my mother's brother, inherited the title from my grandfather. Based on the fabrics and style of the furnishings, I think he must have created this room. It's a long story, but my mother married my father, a vicar, which displeased her father. For a while, my grandfather cut off communications. But when my sister, Lizzie, was young, Grandpapa and Uncle Robert became part of our lives. When Grandpapa died, Uncle Robert inherited, and we never heard from him again—until I was notified that I had inherited his title."

"How did your uncle die?" Wright asked.

"We've heard it was a carriage accident, and I've seen nothing to say otherwise. His solicitor told me he found out weeks after Uncle Robert's passing that he had died, and he needed to provide familial information to assist investigators in locating me. This inheritance is still new to me. I learned about it shortly after leaving Romney's—after the rescue."

"Well, whoever designed this hideaway did an outstanding job," Wright said.

"What did I tell you?" Michael said, pleased at his friend's reaction. The entire room seemed to have been a more recent addition, with almost-new furnishings. The walnut cabinets built into the wall at the end of the room were well stocked, housing an abundance of liquor, and the green card tables gave room for a large party—perfect for the holidays, he thought. "And the centerpiece," he said, pulling off a linen cover from the top of the billiard table, "is my favorite. The table does not look worn in the least. Cue sticks are over there." He pointed to the wall adjacent to the table. "I had the room cleaned, but that was all."

A knock on the sliding wood panel preceded Stanhope's entry. "My lords, I would be happy to bring you some food," he said.

"Would you like anything, Wright?" Michael asked.

Wright gave a sheepish look. "I broke my fast early this morning, so if there's anything light, I'd not complain."

"That sounds like something I could get behind, too. Stanhope, ask Mrs. Peppers to prepare a few sandwiches and a platter of fruit and cheese."

"Consider it done, my lord." Stanhope turned to go, but then turned back, his face reddening. "I almost forgot what else I came here to tell you," the butler said. "Mr. Hastings has asked that I let you know Dr. Enzo Bianchi will be here tomorrow to examine your leg. The good doctor has an office in Amberley and several patients in the area. Mr. Hastings apologized for not having informed you about it earlier." He sniffed.

At the mention of the physician's name, Michael felt a wave of irritation wash over him. The last thing he wanted was the Italian physician insisting on slathering that nasty-smelling salve on his leg.

"Well, the good doctor can examine my leg, but there'll be no talk of applying concoctions," Michael said. He had no interest in smelling like a rotting animal's carcass, especially with Emma and Katie staying there. The salve smelled horrible, and it had been bad enough to subject his servants to it; he wouldn't do that to his guests.

"Yes, my lord," Stanhope said before retreating.

"What's this about concoctions?" Wright asked after the butler had left.

Michael pointed sourly to his leg. "Dr. Bianchi, who is from Italy, has certain notions that he can help heal the scarred tendons in my leg. And Hastings believes him. He concocted a salve that he insists needs to be applied morning and night every day. I admit, it does take the ache out, but the smell is a whole new kind of punishment." Although Michael had to admit—at least to himself—that his limp *had* been improving. That was before the journey from London and the recent mishap in the library. Although the kiss was worth the pain he'd experienced in his leg.

Wright laughed. "I can appreciate that. But if it helps you, don't mind us. I'm sure I've smelled far worse on board a ship that has been at sea with a crew full of men who haven't bathed in months."

"Even so, I doubt you've ever encountered *this* particular smell before—a cross between dead fish and dog excrement. I would have to be in agony before I would subject my guests to that odor," Michael said with a laugh.

"Methinks you would not be so opposed to it if the lovely Lady Emma were not one of your guests." Wright grinned. "Shall we play?"

Michael frowned as Wright passed him a cue stick. His friend was right, but he refused to admit it. "Given that you're my esteemed guest, you may go first."

"Thank you. Red ball, back-left corner," Wright said, tapping the white ball and easily sinking the intended target.

Michael shook his head at the smug grin Wright threw his way. His friend was a self-proclaimed lifelong bachelor. One day, he would meet a woman who would tie him up in knots as Emma did with him. And when that happened, he would relish teasing Wright.

CHAPTER THIRTEEN

That evening

"I'M AFRAID THAT while the master would normally allow Dr. Bianchi to attend him, he refuses to see the doctor because the doctor will want him to use his special salve, and the master refuses to use it—at least while he has guests. And it is that salve that helps his leg and eases his pain," Stanhope said to Hastings, as the two men sat at the table in the kitchen.

Emma stepped completely into the kitchen. She'd overheard the tail end of their conversation and was determined to find out more. "I didn't mean to eavesdrop, but I was walking in and overheard you say Lord Wilton is refusing a doctor's visit. Is it for his leg?"

"Yes, because of the salve the doctor will insist he use," Hastings groaned. "He's the worst when it comes to helping himself with that leg. I shouldn't be telling you this, but the leg bedevils him constantly—the pain is intense. And the only thing we've found to be of any help is the salve prepared by the little Italian doctor from London, who also has a practice here, in the village."

"I see," Emma said, furrowing her brow. "What is his objection to it?"

"The smell," Hastings and Stanhope said together.

"Upon my word! That bad?" Emma asked, startled.

"Yes," Hastings grumbled. "His lordship calls it skunk spray...when he's being polite."

"I heard him compare it to a rotting animal carcass as I was leaving the billiard room earlier today," Stanhope said, grimacing. "I have to agree. He's not far off with that description. Oh, zounds! I apologize, your ladyship, for the language. But the salve is most odiferous."

Emma burst into laughter. "There's no reason to apologize. We're all quite familiar with those smells. Together they create a very colorful description, indeed."

"I had wanted his leg to be of some relief to him on his birthday," muttered Hastings, setting his cup down with a frustrated thump.

"His birthday? When is Lord Wilton's birthday?" Emma asked.

"In a little over a week, on the fourteenth of May. He never remembers his birthday, and he's not one to mark it, either. In all the years I've known him—back when we were in the war—he would always remember the birthdays of his men and get dinner and a mug of ale, or something like it. But when it comes to *his* birthday, he always forgets. Or rather, he opts not to remember."

"He's always been one of those leaders you don't mind taking orders from, if you ken my meaning. He cared about the men under his command in battle," Hastings explained. "And I knew many enlisted boys who were not as lucky as I was to have such a commander in the war."

"And the earl has been a generous lord since he inherited the title," Stanhope agreed. "I'll tell Mrs. Peppers when she returns from the village. She would be terribly upset if she weren't informed about the master's birthday. She'll make him a cake."

"I'm sure Mrs. Peppers will want to do far more than just bake a cake," Hastings drawled. "She'll no doubt plan a special dinner with all his lordship's favorites."

"I think that's a fine idea," Emma said. "We should have a birthday dinner for him. With your help, we can alert the others in the household and make it a lovely celebration."

"We'll make a list of what we'll need, and I'll head into the village early tomorrow morning," Hastings said.

"I'm sure Mrs. Peppers will have a list a mile long to add to it," Stanhope added.

"Splendid!" Emma said. "We have to make sure to keep things a secret from Lord Wilton."

"May I suggest we enlist the assistance of Wright?" Hastings added with a twinkle in his eyes.

"Good idea," Emma said. "I'll make sure to speak with him. And I'll take care of decorating the dining room," she added. "And if I could speak with the Italian doctor, perhaps there is something I can do to help make the salve less noxious." She was thinking about the essence of sandalwood she had seen in one of the linen cabinets. "All right. We all have our duties. I'll ask Katie to create a birthday card. She enjoys drawing."

"If Katie needs any charcoal, paper, or a pencil, I will add it to the list," Stanhope offered. "I'll also check the nursery. There may be drawing instruments in there."

"If we can pull this off, Lord Wilton will be very surprised," Hastings said, much more enthused than when Emma had entered the kitchen. "Dr. Bianchi has an office in town. I'll contact him and ask him to stop by for a quick visit with you. Maybe we can convince Lord Wilton to meet with the good doctor as well, while he's here."

"Perfect! Have him bring some of the salve," Emma suggested.

Hastings and Stanhope laughed together.

"Why are you laughing?" Emma asked.

"No need. I can supply you with some of that now. Lord Wilton has enough salve to last him an entire year!" Hastings replied, wiping tears of laughter from his eyes.

"Why so much?" Emma asked.

"Because every time the good doctor came to visit, he would bring a jar of salve, and Lord Wilton would tell us to lock it up!" Stanhope inserted.

"Last I counted, we had twenty jars. I'll just be a few

minutes," Hastings said.

Emma looked at them and rolled her eyes to the heavens.

"We're not laughing *at* his lordship. It's just the situation because he can be stubborn," Stanhope said.

"Yes, he can be stubborn," Emma muttered.

Hastings returned a few minutes later with a small pot of the salve and handed it to Emma. She lifted the lid and quickly closed it once more. "Phew. His lordship has not exaggerated the smell. It's truly awful," she said. Emma could certainly understand his reluctance to have such a foul-smelling concoction massaged into his leg. Michael was a stoic and proud man, considerate of others, and would not want to offend anyone with his presence, especially a noxious odor that accompanied it. Thinking of his putting up with the terrible pain in his leg to prevent the discomfort of others made her heart wrench.

Michael had stubbornly refused all her attempts to compensate him for the dresses. Emma hoped that the party—and hopefully, a much improved, more tolerable salve—would be a way of thanking him for his generosity.

But this wasn't just about her wanting to show him her gratitude; it was about her concern about his leg. Michael was in so much pain. She'd observed it herself throughout the journey here—surreptitiously, of course. She couldn't help but see the strained look in his eyes or the gray pallor of his face. Or the fact that his limp had become far more pronounced since they'd arrived. She thought about when she fell in the library and he caught her, and her heart squeezed. That had likely made his leg worse.

If there was something she could do to help him, she would. Besides, she preferred his smile to his gruffness. Although his gruffness didn't deter her. But that smile. *Oh, Lord!* When he smiled, that cute little dimple danced on his chin. Not that she would tell him that. But just thinking about it made her face heat with a blush.

All the same, it felt good to be doing something useful. And the idea of helping Michael stirred a feeling of pleasure within her that wrapped around her like a comforting blanket.

"Hastings, do you have any suggestions for a discreet place where I could work on this salve, so the pungent aroma won't spread throughout the house?" she asked, barely able to contain her excitement.

"I do. There's a secluded room tucked away behind the stables that might serve perfectly for your needs," he replied thoughtfully. "And it has a window."

"Perfect..." she said. "I will let you both know the results of my experiment."

"Oh, we'll know if it works," Stanhope said.

"How will you know?" Emma said with a curious smile.

"Why, it won't smell it anymore, will it?" Hastings replied with a chuckle.

Joining in their laughter, she asked Stanhope to prepare some tea and snacks for the modiste and her assistant for later, and then she hurried on her way, glad to have found a way to help Michael with his injured leg. She smiled, thinking about helping to plan a surprise birthday party for the man who was coming to mean so very much to her.

EMMA STEPPED BACK and sighed, smiling as she admired the clock she and Michael had discovered in the attic. It had stopped working, but luckily, Hastings, whose father was a clockmaker, knew how to repair it. And after that, all it needed was a good polish. Its graceful brass case gleamed once more, the delicate hands ticking steadily across an ivory face. Now proudly restored, it sat upon the parlor mantel, a handsome focal point in the room. Emma had decided to focus on refurbishing the rooms that would be used to entertain guests, whether for tea or dinner.

The transformation that the parlor had undergone since their arrival pleased her greatly. The walls had been freshly washed and painted in a gentle, buttery cream, giving the room a soft, comforting warmth. Running her hand down the sleek damask curtains, she marveled at how lovely they looked, having been fashioned from the surprisingly well-preserved fabric they'd also found packed away in a trunk. She loved how the rich azure blue of the curtains on the wide, multi-paned windows complemented the soothing shade of the walls. An elegant, ornate secretaire made of mahogany, which they'd also found in the attic's treasure trove, had been cleaned and polished and now sat beneath one of the windows on the far side of the room.

Glancing at her list in the small bound notebook she'd begun to carry around with her, she noted that the new Axminster carpet in a darker hue of blue was due to be delivered tomorrow, along with the settee that had been re-covered in a cheery floral pattern that matched the blue of the drapes and the pale yellow of the walls. And then the room would be complete.

Taking one last look around the room, she sighed, pleased with their efforts in the parlor. Leaving the room, she noticed the quiet of the house. Michael was with the stonemason and several workers hired to repair the wall bordering the estate. Katie was upstairs, likely taking a nap by now, under the supervision of Doris. It would be a perfect time to experiment with the salve.

Emma retrieved the jar of salve and the small vials of sandalwood oil and orange essence she had tucked away in a box off the kitchen, along with a kerchief and other utensils she might need. She knew that Michael favored sandalwood and citrus soap and shaving cream. If she could use enough to mask the pungent odor of the salve, maybe he wouldn't mind using it.

Easily finding the room at the far end of the stables, she unlatched the wooden shutter and used a sturdy piece of wood to keep it open. She'd used a cask she'd found in the corner, rolling it over to the door to ensure it stayed open as well. Hopefully, between the open window and door, enough air would flow through the room, and the smell would not be as overwhelming.

Tying the kerchief over her nose and mouth, Emma divided the salve into three equal measures, which she spooned into three separate glass jars. In the first, she blended several drops of sandalwood oil and mixed it thoroughly; in the second, she used both the essence of orange and sandalwood, and in the third, she added only the orange essence. After each mixture, she wrote in her notebook how many drops she had used of each oil, along with approximately how much salve she had used.

As she finished blending the salve with the mixture of orange and sandalwood, she heard a soft *woof* and suddenly found herself sharing the room with Finn, who began to sniff the air below each jar.

"Woof!" he barked more loudly when he sniffed below the one that had the orange and sandalwood a second, then a third time.

She tugged down the kerchief that had covered her nose and mouth and sniffed the jar Finn had barked at, before sniffing the other two. "You approve of this one?" she asked, happy to have an opinion, even if it was from a dog. Finn wagged his tail and barked once more. She couldn't detect any of the original salve's smell, and while she had added orange essence, it seemed to enhance the sandalwood, not overpower it. "It does smell lovely," she said to the dog, patting his head. "Maybe this will work, after all."

Earlier, as she made her way to the stables made her way to the stables, she'd noticed Finn in the company of Michael and Wright. They had likely been laboring alongside the craftsmen from town, diligently working on the wall. She imagined how exhausting the task must have been, especially under the warm sun. Knowing the physical demands of their work, she felt a pang of concern for Michael. He would be tired and sore after such strenuous labor. Perhaps Hastings would be able to give him a soothing massage with the improved salve.

"Now, what brings you in here, Finn? I'm afraid I don't have any treats in my pockets for you," she said, stepping outside the door and looking around, before stepping back inside. No apples to be found either. "Did you decide the work on the wall wasn't appealing enough to keep you amused, dear boy?"

"Woof," he repeated, nudging the middle jar containing the salve that had been mixed with both essential oils.

"I take it that means you like it. I do, too. The question is whether Michael will approve," she said, kissing Finn on the nose.

"Approve of what?" a familiar, deep voice said.

Emma looked up as Michael walked into the room. "It smells good in here," he said, reaching down and scratching Finn behind the ears. "What is it?" He leaned down and sniffed the jars. "It smells like sandalwood."

"It is sandalwood and orange, actually," she said, pleased that he liked the scent.

"Is this some concoction you're using to wax the furniture in the parlor?" he asked with a curious smile.

"Er...no..." She swallowed, suddenly nervous at revealing her true purpose. "I, um, asked Hastings for a jar of the salve that Dr. Bianchi had compounded for your leg. I thought, perhaps, we could mask the odor. I...well, I hoped—"

"You what?" he interrupted, his tone tinged with irritation, his eyes narrowing.

"I-I wanted to surprise you. I wanted to help. I thought if the salve didn't have such a noxious odor that you might not be so averse to using it, and it could help with your leg."

"Are you a physician now?" he said in a sharp tone. "You think a few drops of scented oil will be the magical cure for this mangled leg?"

"No," she replied, shocked at his words and his sudden flash of anger. "It's only that after our journey here, your leg seemed to pain you even more, and then it seemed to get even worse since the night in the library when you fell and hurt your leg."

"I'm not hurt," he responded tersely. "And I didn't fall. I was preventing *you* from falling and injuring yourself when you foolishly climbed up that ladder in the dark."

She felt her face flush with embarrassment at his reprimand. Even more so because the kiss that followed after he'd indeed broken her fall was emblazoned in her mind. "I was only trying to help," she whispered brokenly.

Feeling her eyes blur with tears and her bottom lip quiver, she gathered the two vials of essential oils, corked them, and shoved them back into her pocket. "I need to check on Katie. Please excuse me." Without another word or glance in his direction, she whirled and rushed out the door, unable to stem the flow of tears running down her cheeks, and unwilling to allow him to view her mortification.

CHAPTER FOURTEEN

"**D**AMN AND BLAST!" Michael muttered, running his fingers through his hair. "I didn't mean to hurt her." Frustrated, he watched her walk toward the manor house through the open window in the stable room.

Finn looked up at him and growled, something the normally happy-go-lucky dog never did. And did Finn just shake his head at him?

"I know. I'm an idiot," he said.

Finn cocked his head and gave an indignant woof.

"I deserve that *and* the pain I'm experiencing," Michael said as he bent to rub his leg. Working on rebuilding the crumbled parts of the wall over the past two days had only compounded the twisting pain in his thigh. "It seems even my bloody leg agrees."

Finn nudged the middle jar with his nose and barked.

"You want me to smell it?" he said, picking up the jar. Michael smiled as he inhaled the pleasant aroma of sandalwood with subtle hints of orange. Not overpowering at all. "My God, she did it." She had fixed the salve, making the scent pleasing. It smelled fresh, not foul. "She did this for me," he said with wonder. He wouldn't have a problem using the salve now, but he had no idea how to replicate it once he ran out. Knowing Emma, she'd probably written it down. He'd have to ask her for the recipe.

After he apologized.

Why had he reacted the way he did? He'd humiliated her. He'd hurt her. And all she was trying to do was help him. *She did all of this for me, and I practically bit her head off.*

He'd seen the tears, the quivering lip, the hurt in her eyes just before she looked away and ran out of the stable.

I'm such a fool.

He'd let his pride take over, and now he'd hurt Emma…

Since his return to Society, he'd feigned indifference when it came to his injury and his very visible limp. He'd acted as though he were unaffected because that was what men did. Society tended to look down on war veterans who'd returned from battle with injuries, whether they were visible or invisible. A friend of his, a fellow officer, and a second son to a duke, had come home minus an arm and blind in one eye. His young wife had screamed and fainted when she saw him. Since that day, they'd resided in separate homes. He stayed at his country estate. She stayed in London.

Despite Michael's stoic strength and declaration that he'd rather not attend *ton* functions because of the frivolous nature of debutantes and their overbearing, matchmaking mamas—especially now that he was an earl—he'd been expected to attend balls, but he doubted anyone would appreciate his dragging his leg across the dance floor. Before he had been captured and tortured, he had been a very capable dancer. Some women had even gushed about his ability to practically glide across the dance floor. But no more. His pronounced limp ensured he would be the least appealing partner for any *ton* event. Realizing this, he'd avoided Society. It was part of the reason he'd left London. If he weren't there, no one would invite him.

Deep down he didn't think he would ever meet a woman who wouldn't be shocked or, worse, feel revulsion over his twisted and scarred leg. For that reason, he had decided never to marry. He couldn't. No woman would want a man with a mangled leg that would require attention when the pain became unbearable.

And then he'd met Emma.

His thoughts turned to that memorable morning in the attic. Together, they had sifted through every trunk and looked at every piece of furniture, searching for the perfect items that would help them restore the neglected beauty of the manor house. They'd talked excitedly about the memorabilia and trinkets they found, guessing what they might have meant to those original occupants. Her enthusiasm had been infectious and seemingly driven by a desire to please him. He recalled the wedding veil she'd found and how his thoughts had taken flight, imagining her wearing that veil as she walked down the aisle toward him.

Last night, he'd dreamed he was twirling Emma around a gleaming ballroom floor, where crystal chandeliers sparkled like stars against a beautiful moonlit sky. He'd pictured her in an exquisite pink gown, the very one he had seen her wearing earlier that afternoon. Her brilliant smile had lit up the room, and her gorgeous violet eyes had gazed adoringly up at him, glowing with wonderment and joy, as if he were the only man in the world. He closed his eyes once more, and he could almost feel her presence, her intoxicating, sweet jasmine scent enveloping his senses like a warm embrace, stirring desires and emotions from deep within his heart—emotions unlike anything he had ever felt.

He held up the jar once more and inhaled the subtle fragrance.

He had to make this right.

He replayed his words—his tone, his dismissive attitude, and his accusation that she didn't like the smell. *Hell!* No one liked the smell, most especially him. After all, who wanted to smell like a dead animal allowed to lie fallow in the sun for days?

"We have to fix this, Finn," he said, looking down at the dog and rubbing its head. "You should have stopped me from making such an arse of myself."

The dog cocked his head to the side and gave him a quizzical look.

"I know. It's not your mess. But perhaps you can take pity on me and help me."

His traitorous dog yawned.

"So, I see that's a no," Michael said, raising an eyebrow. "Honestly, Finn, I can't blame you. But look what I have." He took a small biscuit from his pocket and handed it to the dog, who, rather than take it like he usually did, stared at it as if Michael had asked him to dance. "It's not a bribe," he added quickly.

Finn blinked but didn't take the biscuit, as if Michael had handed the dog a plate of cooked spinach.

How am I going to fix this? Stuffing the biscuit back in his pocket, he began to walk away, and a tightness gripped his heart. Doubts clouded his mind as he pondered what to do. The weight of uncertainty felt like a familiar yoke around his neck, and the fear of failure and embarrassment loomed over him. Each step he took felt heavier.

I need to do something, but what? And can I repair this without making it worse?

CHAPTER FIFTEEN

The next day

"THE STONEMASONS HAVE repaired the worst parts of the wall that were crumbling," Michael said, pointing to three different sections on the drawings he'd laid out on the billiard table.

"Good idea to add five feet in height," Wright said. "It'll provide more privacy as well as deterrence. Like you, I'm hoping the project will be completed quickly."

"Indeed," Michael said. "They are working swiftly and efficiently. Thank you for recommending Bradford."

"He's exceptional, and his apprentices are as hardworking as he is," Wright agreed.

"My lords, forgive the intrusion," Stanhope said from the open wall panel that connected the gaming room to the study.

Michael looked up from the plans and stood. "Not a problem, Stanhope."

"Lord Wright, your aunt, Lady Margaret Chipperly, has arrived along with a Mr. Craig Burns."

Michael glanced at Wright. "This should be interesting," he quipped, arching a brow.

Wright groaned in frustration, raking his hands through his hair. "I love my aunt dearly, but she just can't resist interfering. She said nothing when we discussed Mr. Burns's coming to interview Lady Emma and Katie," he said.

"One might think she feels a sense of ownership." Michael snickered, clearly amused. "Show them to the drawing room, Stanhope, and please inform Lady Emma. We'll be there shortly."

Emma hadn't said a word to Michael since he had spoken so ruthlessly to her in the stable. She had avoided him at dinner, sending Stanhope word that she was turning in early and choosing to have dinner in her room. This morning, she'd avoided the breakfast room as well. Michael had been tempted to knock on her door to apologize and beg her forgiveness. But Wright had arrived back from checking on his ship and his men and they'd thrown themselves into a discussion on the plans for the walls and other necessary repairs around the estate. They hadn't expected the artist to arrive until tomorrow. Clearly, Lady Chipperly had hurried things along. He still needed to apologize to Emma, but it would be even more difficult with a house full of people.

"Very good, my lord. I will ask Mrs. Peppers to prepare tea and a light repast," the retainer said, his lips twitching as he turned to leave, uncharacteristically trying to hide a smile.

"Is your aunt by chance acquainted with Lady Beadle?" Michael asked his friend as he began to roll up the designs they had been examining.

"Are they *acquainted*?" Wright snorted. "They are lifelong rivals. Ever since their first London Season forty-five years ago!"

"Well, we might have a bit of a conundrum, then," Michael said.

"Why?"

"Armstrong sent word last evening that he'd just arrived at his estate along with Celia and Lady Beadle. They plan to stop by today to update us on the investigation."

"Good God!" Wright replied, running his hands through his hair again. "This has disaster written all over it."

"I'm certain that both Lady Beadle and Lady Chipperly understand the importance of the situation."

"Would you like to wager on that?"

Michael chuckled. "No, my friend. But I think between all of us, we can keep them from dueling on the front lawn."

"Welcome, Lady Chipperly," Michael said a few minutes later after Wright had made the introductions. "Wright has told me a great deal about you." Michael smiled as he lifted her gloved hand and kissed it. "I feel as though I already know you."

"Please, call me Aunt Chippie!" the older woman gushed.

"Aunt Chippie, this is a surprise," Wright said. "I thought you were spending a few days entertaining your friend Julia."

"Humph! That woman…" Aunt Chippie frowned. "Julia and I had words, and she left to return to London a few days early."

Wright exchanged an amused look with Michael over his aunt's head.

"It was all for the best in any case, wasn't it, dear Mr. Burns?" she said with a flirtatious smile at the artist, who looked to be about twenty years younger.

"Quite right, my lady." Burns smiled at Aunt Chippie.

Michael noted it was a polite and somewhat patient smile. Burns appeared to be a respectful man with no ulterior motives. Wright had told him he had already looked into the artist's background and found him to be completely genuine and truly dedicated to his art.

"Of course, I insisted that Mr. Burns use my carriage rather than the stagecoach. And then I had the most brilliant idea. All very last-minute, you see. I thought that I might be of some use or assistance. At the very least, I could provide feminine guidance to your lovely young guests. I do hope I am not *de trop*, am I?"

"On the contrary, my lady, you are most welcome. I have already instructed Stanhope to prepare two guest rooms." Michael smiled.

"Oh, you are most kind, Lord Wilton."

"Please call me Michael, my lady."

"Well, you must call me Aunt Chippie."

"Thank you, Aunt Chippie," Michael said.

"How did you find the journey here, Aunt?" Wright asked.

"Quite comfortable, nary a bump in the road. Was that not so, Mr. Burns?"

"Indeed, the journey was most comfortable, thanks to Lady Chipperly's generosity," the artist said with a smile. "But truthfully, I am eager to begin. When Lord Wright spoke to me of the gravity of this matter, along with the delicacy of a child being involved as a witness, I said yes, immediately. I am at your service, my lords. If you'll show me where you'd like me to set up, I can begin as soon as it's convenient for you."

"Perhaps by the window?" Michael suggested.

Burns turned to regard the large picture window where sunlight streamed in. "Yes, it will afford us plenty of light. If you will allow me to retrieve my tools from the carriage."

"Of course," Michael said, nodding at one of the footmen to assist the artist.

He stopped speaking as Lady Beadle and the Armstrongs entered the room.

The footman returned a few minutes later carrying an easel, followed by Burns, who carried a large sketchpad and a box of what no doubt contained charcoal and other accoutrements of his craft. As Michael directed them to the window, he heard a familiar, melodious voice, and turned to see Emma enter the drawing room, holding Katie's hand. Stanhope must have told her the artist had arrived, given the stoic look on her face and her squared shoulders.

Katie tugged on her aunt's hand. The child was trembling. Emma crouched and spoke softly to her niece. Katie nodded and gave her a tremulous smile. Michael swallowed the lump in his throat as he watched Emma hug the little girl. He'd worried about the effect this exercise would have on Katie, having to relive that horrific night when they'd barely escaped with their lives. The child hadn't had a nightmare in several days, but after this, would she experience a setback? His heart wrenched at the thought.

Michael made a move toward them, but in the same moment, Aunt Chippie turned and let out a squeal of delight. "Oh, what darlings!" she exclaimed as she hurried toward Emma and Katie.

Wright glanced at Michael with an arched brow, and Michael nodded for him to make the introductions.

After that was done, Emma and Katie sat on armchairs that had been placed in front of the window next to Burns, who sat with his back to the window, facing his easel. A small table had been placed next to the easel, holding the box of drawing tools.

Emma had been polite but cool toward Michael. Of course, he deserved it, given that he'd behaved like an ass. But what caused his heart to hurt was seeing her eyes slightly red and swollen. She'd been crying, and it was his fault. He wanted to do something, but this wasn't the time.

Aunt Chippie was perched on an armchair that she insisted be placed next to the artist. Despite Wright's attempts to encourage her to sit on the settee, she had insisted on seating herself beside Burns. "I might be able to offer some guidance, you see," she said.

Burns did not seem to mind and appeared intently focused on his work. Michael suppressed a smile as he realized the artist probably had a great deal of patience for Aunt Chippie, given that she was his greatest patron and had no doubt helped him gain many new clients.

"My lord, Lord and Lady Armstrong and Lady Beadle have arrived," Stanhope said as he entered, and then stepped aside to admit the trio.

Aunt Chippie gasped as she turned to the new arrivals.

"Fancy seeing you here, Chippie. I thought you couldn't bear to leave your beloved Brighton?" Lady Beadle said.

"Millie, I see you haven't lost your penchant for insults. I am here to offer my assistance."

Michael and Wright quickly stepped into the fray, greeting their friends warmly and explaining the situation.

Lady Beadle and Celia hugged Emma and Katie warmly.

"I'm so happy to see you both," Lady Beadle said. "How are you faring?"

"Very well," Emma said, smiling down at Katie.

Katie hugged her doll close to her chest and gave a shy smile.

"I am glad we arrived when we did," Lady Beadle said.

Armstrong pulled Michael and Wright aside to his study for a private chat, away from Emma and Katie. "The fire at Lady Beadle's seems to have been deliberately started," he explained. "I saw a few people hanging around, but they were probably just curious. Most of the crowd jumped in to help quickly. There's a chance *he* was involved, but it doesn't match his usual arson style. The fire was quite small, and I think if he did start it, he was after something. Since it was set in the carriage house and was quickly extinguished."

"I'd like to delay telling Emma until later, and certainly not in front of Katie," Michael said.

"I agree," Armstrong said. "I've already asked Celia and Lady Beadle not to speak of it here, especially not with Katie around."

Once they had agreed, the three men returned to join the ladies.

Aunt Chippie and Lady Beadle were both staring daggers at each other.

"I heard that the widow, Lady Chapin, is marrying Lord Bucknell. He was best friends with Arthur, was he not?" Aunt Chippie asked.

"I would hardly say they were friends," Lady Beadle said with a huff. "*My dearest Author* was a man of great intellect and was hardly friends with Lord Bucknell, who spends most of his days gambling, when he's not chasing wealthy widows. I heard he'd gone to Brighton for several weeks to pay you court, dear Chippie." Lady Beadle flippantly pointed her cane at Chippie.

"That is a lie. I would never allow myself to be courted by the likes of Lord Bucknell. Now, Arthur, on the other hand, was a true gentleman and courted me for several months before you lured him away."

Lady Beadle gasped at the insult. "Lured him away? I beg your pardon. My dear Arthur had eyes for me and only me ever since my debut in Society. And you should remember that, since it was the Everly ball that was your debut as well."

"Ha! So, you say," Aunt Chippie snapped back. "But I recall something entirely different, a bouquet of flowers that Arthur brought me the next day."

"You created a fantasy in your mind, dear Chippie. Firstly, I asked Arthur to give you flowers so that you wouldn't be hurt by all the bouquets that I received from my admirers."

"Oh, that is low, even for you, Millie," Aunt Chippie countered.

"And secondly, he brought you flowers…once," Lady Beadle continued. "Your house was on the way to my house. It was the day after our debut. That was all. He was merely dropping off the flowers on his way to my house. He told me. Besides, they were pink snapdragons."

Aunt Chippie's eyes widened. "He told you that he brought me snapdragons?"

"Of course… And you *do* know what snapdragons stand for, don't you?" At Chippie's silent frown, Lady Beadle continued. "They stand for deviousness. Even my dear Arthur had you pegged," she concluded in a tone that brooked no forbearance.

"Oh! Is that what you think? I'll have you know they also mean grace and strength—two things that I have in abundance," Aunt Chippie returned.

"There's quite a history between these two," Michael overheard Celia whisper to Emma as the two dowagers traded insults. "They were friends once, but they became bitter rivals after their come-out. Lord Arthur Beadle did send flowers to both, as well as several other young ladies. Ultimately, it was my aunt whom he pursued. Other young men were competing for their affections, yet it was Uncle Arthur who captured my aunt's heart."

"But they are both widows and could use each other's friendship," Emma whispered back.

"Yes. Once, they were the best of friends...since leading strings, I understand," Celia said.

"Perhaps they could be friends once again?" Emma suggested.

"Perhaps we should get started," Wright and Michael said at the same time. Then they looked at each other with brows raised.

Lord Armstrong cleared his throat. "Lady Chipperly and Lady Beadle—perhaps we should let Mr. Burns begin with his sketch. It could help us in our investigation, which I think we should all keep in mind."

⇥⟫⟫⟪⟪⇤

"KATIE, ARE YOU ready to get started?" Emma asked her niece in a gentle voice.

Katie nodded. "I am, Auntie. But is it all right if Finn is with me, too?"

As she asked, Finn trotted into the drawing room and lay down on the floor at her feet.

Michael's lips twitched at Finn's show of loyalty and support to the little girl. There was no doubt the dog was crazy about Katie. "You can stay, Finn, if you promise to behave."

"Woof!" the dog agreed.

"It's very nice to meet you, Katie," Burns said, smiling at the child. "That's a pretty name. Is it short for something?"

Katie was quiet.

"That's a very nice doll," he continued, trying again. "What's her name?"

Katie looked at her doll's face and kissed her on the nose. "This is Polly. And she's a very good dolly."

"I'm pleased to meet you, Polly. Would it be all right if I asked for your help?"

Katie held Polly up to her ear and then nodded solemnly. "Polly said she would like to help."

"Thank you, Polly," Burns said in a gentle voice. "Polly, do you recall seeing a stranger the night of that fire at your house?"

Katie held Polly up again to her ear, then she turned and whispered in the doll's ear. "Polly said she remembers seeing a man in the yard. Someone she had never seen before. We call him the bad man."

"I see," Burns said. "Can you ask Polly if she remembers what color the bad man's hair was?"

Katie consulted the doll once more and then said, "It was dark."

"Thank you. And was his hair curly or straight?" Burns asked.

"Polly said curly."

"Very good. And can you ask Polly if he had big, round eyes or small, beady eyes?"

Once again, Katie answered on behalf of her doll.

Michael was impressed by the artist's thoughtful approach with Katie. He continued to ask simple questions about each feature, and Katie continued to answer on behalf of Polly.

It took almost an hour of gentle patience, but Burns finally completed the sketch.

Emma asked Katie if she would like to visit Mrs. Peppers in the kitchen for a treat. Katie nodded and smiled, hugging Polly close to her.

"Can Finn come too?" she asked.

Emma looked at Michael, who smiled. "Yes, of course Finn can go too. I'm sure he would enjoy a treat, wouldn't you, boy?" He scratched his dog behind the ears.

"Doris, could you please take Katie and Finn to the kitchen for a snack?" Emma asked.

"Yes, my lady," Doris said, taking Katie's hand. "Come along, dear."

Katie took a few steps forward, then turned back to Burns. "Polly wants to say thank you, Mr. Burns."

"You are very welcome, Polly and Katie," he said warmly.

"I didn't want to upset Katie by showing her the finished sketch," Emma explained after Katie and Doris had left.

"But you also got a look at him?" Michael asked.

Emma nodded, biting her lower lip.

Michael clenched his teeth, feeling a deep desire to hold Emma and comfort her. She was incredibly strong and brave for Katie, yet she was also dealing with her own pain. The bastard was out there, and Michael was certain of it. For reasons he couldn't fully understand, he sensed that Emma was in real danger from this man. She had seen him, and the arsonist had already taken two lives. His fires had gotten bigger and deadlier.

Burns spent a few more minutes on the drawing, then said, "May I show you the finished sketch?"

Michael looked at Emma. "Emma?"

She nodded.

"Is this him?" Burns asked, holding the sketchpad up to Emma.

She gasped. "Yes. My God. That *is* him!" She looked at Michael, her eyes filled with fear, her face so pale that he thought she might faint.

"Water, please," Michael said, swiftly moving to her side and crouching by her chair. Taking her hand, he chafed it between his own.

Celia poured a glass of water and handed it to Emma. "Take a few sips," she said gently, taking the empty seat next to her.

Emma sipped the water and then took a slow, deep breath. "I'm all right. Thank you."

Michael stood and asked to see the sketch. He perused the image but didn't recognize the man depicted. "Armstrong, Wright, do you recognize him?" He passed the sketch to his friends.

"My God! I *do* know this man," Armstrong said. "It's been nagging at me for a while now."

"Who is he?" Wright asked.

"May I see?" Lady Beadle said, making her way to their side. Armstrong handed her the sketch. "Good Lord! I know that man. He's the spitting image of his late father."

"Wait, allow me," Aunt Chippie said, clearly not wanting to be left out. "If Millie recognizes him, I will as well."

Lady Beadle huffed but made room for Aunt Chippie. Armstrong held up the sketch.

"Oh my. Oh dear!" Aunt Chippie said, exchanging a worried glance with Lady Beadle.

"Who is it?" Michael said, his jaw clenched. This was turning into a parlor game.

"Lord Morgrave," Armstrong said in a grim voice. "I haven't seen him in at least a year."

"We knew his father, Viscount Hugh Morgrave," Lady Beadle said.

"The earl was a very popular man back in the day," Chippie said. "He was one of the most sought-after bachelors in London. Do you recall, Millie?"

"Many a young lady vied for his attention. Not me, of course."

"Well, not me, either," Chippie echoed, flipping open a small fan attached to her wrist and fanning herself. "What no one knew was that he was a gambler who lost his family's entire fortune. Not only that, but he also frequented many houses of ill repute."

"What happened to his son?" Wright asked.

"The viscount's wife took their young son to Scotland to live with her family," Lady Beadle said. "After they lost the townhouse. They'd already lost all the unentailed properties. Their estate home had been neglected and fell into disrepair."

"What happened to the viscount?" Emma asked, her voice trembling. Celia wrapped a supportive arm around her shoulders.

Michael wished he could do that for her. He cleared his throat.

Aunt Chippie and Lady Beadle exchanged a glance. "He died destitute at St. Bartholomew's Hospital of a terrible disease—I'm sure you can guess, which one," Lady Beadle said gravely.

Syphilis, Michael thought.

Burns handed Michael a second sketch that looked identical to the first one. "I'll take one of these sketches with me back to London first thing tomorrow and notify all the authorities," he said, carefully folding the drawing and slipping it into his coat.

"By all accounts, the apple may not have fallen far from the tree," Lady Beadle said.

"Opium," Aunt Chippie added.

"We already knew we were dealing with a dangerous man," Michael said. "Now that we know who he is, we need to find him before he strikes again."

CHAPTER SIXTEEN

The next day

EMMA SAT IN the chair in her room, staring at the fire waning in her fireplace. Her head was spinning. So many thoughts churned in her head. So many feelings swirled in her heart. Burns's efforts the night before had miraculously produced a drawing of the man who had burned her sister's home. The home that she and Katie had barely escaped with their lives. Last night, Emma found out the arsonist had retaliated against Lady Beadle for sheltering Emma and Katie, burning her prized carriage house.

Thank God no one was hurt, and Lady Beadle's house was mostly untouched. Lady Beadle had assured her over and over that everyone was fine.

She thought about the drawing. *It's him. I'll never forget that evil smirk. And his eyes were like black pits—soulless.* Even though she'd only glimpsed the man briefly, she was certain that the shadowy figure who'd watched her and Katie the night of the fire was him. She'd felt it down deep in her bones.

Being at Michael's estate these past few weeks had made her and Katie feel safe, and like the fire had been a distant memory. Everyone had made them feel welcome. Emma had been so busy helping with the refurbishing efforts, and Katie was thriving with the devoted Finn by her side. The bond that had formed between them was almost magical. It gave Emma such happiness to watch them.

But when she'd set eyes on that sketch, it had all come rushing back to her full force, throwing her back to that night. The fear. The terror. The danger.

And when her eyes met Michael's, all she wanted to do was to feel his arms around her. But that was not to be. Certainly not in front of all those people, and definitely not after their argument the other day. He had lashed out at her when all she had tried to do was mask the odor of the salve so it could help him. She could see the remorse in his eyes. But, well…remorse was not an apology.

Emma stood and walked to the hearth, stoking the fire to a low flame, before returning to her chair. *He's out there, and he knows what Katie and I look like. And now, we know exactly what he looks like.* She could not help the shiver of fear that coursed through her.

She no longer felt safe at Michael's estate.

Burns's sketch was more than just a drawing; it served as a reminder of the smoke that stung her lungs that night, the frantic chaos of their escape. Now, the arsonist had a face, filling in the missing piece of the nightmare crafted by that flesh-and-blood madman. And he had a name—Viscount Gideon Morgrave.

A shudder skittered up her spine.

"Lady Beadle's fire was small in comparison to the others," Lord Armstrong had said last night as he'd spoken in hushed tones with Wright and Michael. Emma had overheard them speaking in Michael's study on her way back from checking on Katie.

"He may have used the fire as a way to drive Lady Beadle away from London…" Armstrong had added.

"You mean to say he might have used the fire as a ruse to follow you to Sussex?" Michael had said in a steely voice.

"We were very careful on the journey," Armstrong had said calmly. "But I am concerned. We need to be even more vigilant."

"What a bastard," Wright had said.

"I heard him that night at the inn," Armstrong had continued.

"His lies were smooth and compelling. Had we not already been able to count the innkeeper and his wife as reliable informants, I don't think your escape would have gone as smoothly."

Emma replayed the conversation in her mind while staring into the crackling flames in the hearth. Had the arsonist followed the Armstrongs and Lady Beadle here?

Feeling an overwhelming sense of panic come over her, she got up from her chair, wanting to go check on Katie again, even though she'd checked only twenty minutes ago. She had to find her niece.

She jerked the bedroom door open and came face to face with Michael, holding a bouquet of jasmine vines and white roses.

"I came to apologize," he said.

She looked at him, words rolling through her mind, but unsure of what to say. "I...I must check on Katie," she said, clinging to the thought she'd had before opening the door.

He made no effort to move. "I just checked on her. Finn was snoring up a storm, and I poked my head into her room. Doris is there as well, sleeping on the bed next to her."

Emma felt her panic deflate a little.

"Please. You must hear me out," he implored her, holding out the bouquet. "I just need a few minutes of your time."

"You hurt me," she forced out.

"I know. And I'm sorry," he whispered, his voice hoarse. "Hastings called me a fool when I told him."

"You...you told Hastings? she asked. If Hastings knew, then she suspected Stanhope and Mrs. Peppers likely knew as well. Her humiliation complete, her face heated with embarrassment. Everyone would know he'd scolded her as though she were an errant child.

"Yes. Or rather, he guessed. Hastings and I have been friends for twelve years, in good times and bad. He always speaks his mind when I need it. He is my valet, but he's also one of my closest friends and has been since the war. He saved my life. Please don't get upset about his knowing; he guessed that something had happened." He held the bouquet out to her. "I picked these myself, with you in mind." His face was flushed as he cleared his throat. "These two flowers made me think of you…fragrant and lovely," he said.

She finally took the bouquet and lifted it to her nose, inhaling deeply.

She knew he was waiting for an answer. His eyes looked so hopeful.

She wanted to say yes. The word was on the tip of her tongue.

His compliment had been so sincere and so unexpected that she needed to adjust to the surprise. Never had she been given her flowers with such sincerity. His gruff manner was gone, and he looked like a boy waiting to be forgiven for having broken a window.

She held the bouquet to her nose once again, hiding a smile. No one had ever given her jasmine and white roses. It was a beautiful bouquet.

"What I said was unforgivable, Emma. The way I treated you…" He shook his head, as if disgusted with himself. "I lost my head and said things I didn't mean. I have no defense. All I can say is that your simple gesture made me feel exposed. I'm a man with fears and hurts that I try to hide," he said. "I behaved badly."

"What do you mean, exposed?"

He blew out a breath. "I mean, this injury… It changed me." He paused to look down at his leg, then gestured to her room. "Would it be all right if I step inside? I promise to behave myself." He gave that smile of his, the one with the irresistible dimple.

She hesitated at first, then nodded and stepped aside so that he could enter her room.

He turned to close the door, but not all the way, leaving it slightly ajar. He turned back to her and cleared his throat again. "I was a young man when I first went to war. I was physically strong. I was an excellent shot. I was a strong fighter. I felt invincible, just as many young men feel when they first go to war.

But war changes all that, especially when you see dear friends die on the battlefield or go home with a missing limb or completely blind as a result of their injuries... I was one of the lucky ones. And yet, at first, I refused to see that, refused to be thankful. I also refused to see how my injury had changed my life...how it had changed me." He gave a rueful, crooked smile. "It turns out, I was never invincible."

She swallowed the lump in her throat, her heart wrenching at the thought of the handsome young man—a boy, really—who went to war full of youthful idealism and bravado, only to be changed by the brutality of battle.

"But what I went through, and how it affected me, is no excuse for how I treated you. For how I lashed out at you. My tirade was cruel and demeaning. And for that, I am truly sorry." He looked down for a moment, then back up again, and his eyes met hers with an open vulnerability she had never seen before. "The salve... I don't know how you did it exactly, but you masked the odor. Even Finn thought so." He chuckled.

She couldn't help but giggle along. "Which one? I mean, which jar?" she asked.

"I don't usually think about what scents I prefer"—he laughed again—"but I'm partial to the second jar you left on the table in the backroom of the stables. The middle jar. I detected sandal-wood and a citrusy orange scent."

That had been her favorite scent, too. Emma started to smile but felt her bottom lip quiver slightly. She bit her lip to hold back the tears. She wanted to be able to speak her mind without falling into a blubbering mess. His nearness stirred those contradictory feelings inside her—warmth and comfort on one hand and a heart-pounding, breathless feeling on the other.

"I'm feeling out of sorts, Lord Wilton. The last day or two has shaken me quite a bit," she finally said.

"Lord Wilton, again. What happened to calling me Michael? I'm sincerely trying to apologize to you. I was so wrong to say the things I did. I didn't mean them. Say you'll try to forgive me."

"Very well, Michael," she said softly. "I accept your apology, and I forgive you. I also regret my actions, running off as I did. I should have stayed to explain or to ask you why you were so angry. And I thank you for the flowers—they are lovely. I'll put them in a vase of water." She started to close the door, and he stopped it.

"I tried the salve last night," he managed to say to the slight crack he had maintained.

"Did it work?" she asked, pleased.

"Do you smell a dead skunk?" he quipped.

"No." She giggled.

"Then it worked."

"Silly man… I mean, does your leg feel better?"

"Oh," he said with a wink. "Yes, it feels *infinitely* better. Hastings will be applying the salve every evening. I hope you will let him know the magical concoction you used to transform the salve."

"It will be my pleasure to do so," she said, feeling a surge of warmth.

"In fact, I might even ask that persistent Italian physician to examine my leg in a month to see if there has been any improvement, and I have you to thank for that."

"Thank you. It's such good news. I am very happy to hear it," she said with a smile.

"I am so happy to see you smile again," he said.

She felt her cheeks blush.

"I also wanted to speak to you about Morgrave," he said, his tone turning serious.

She nodded, trying to tamp down the jolt of panic that had latched on to her earlier.

"I want to reassure you, Emma, that we will find him," Michael said, taking a step closer to her, where she stood next to the fireplace. "That is my promise to you. My pledge. We know what he looks like, we know who he is. Armstrong has already sent a missive to headquarters in London, along with the sketch."

"I have something to confess…"

"Oh?"

"I…um…I overheard your speaking with Wright and Armstrong in your study. That Morgrave may have set that fire at Lady Beadle's home to force her to leave and lead him here…"

He nodded. "Armstrong didn't think about the possibility of Morgrave using them until they were almost here. By then, he decided that perhaps we should look at this differently. We know what the arsonist looks like, and we're pretty sure we know who he is. But he doesn't know that we know all of that. We plan to go on the offensive and look for him. That includes here. We are showing everyone in my security force his picture. I promise to keep you safe."

She began to tremble at the thought of Morgrave being out there, nearby.

Michael reached out and clasped her shoulders. "I'm going to do everything in my power to keep you and Katie safe, Emma. Do you trust me?"

She didn't immediately answer him.

His brow furrowed. "Everything seems so stiff and formal between us. Only days ago, we were laughing and even holding hands," he said, picking up her hand. When she drew back, he dropped it. "I'm not going to take advantage—even though every part of me wants to kiss you."

"Yes, I do trust you," she whispered. "But Morgrave has escaped detection for so long. It's like he's a ghost, able to do all these terrible things without being caught. Without being seen."

"But he *was* seen. By you and Katie. And it is because of your courage that he will be caught. I promise you. I will protect you with my life."

"I want to believe you, Michael. But I'm scared…for me and Katie," she whispered. "I don't want you to lose your life trying to protect me." Her eyes were blurring with tears.

"Please, Emma," he rasped. "I can't bear to see you cry."

With a groan, he pulled her into his arms and held her tight.

For a moment, she allowed herself to imagine how wonderful it would be to feel his arms around her every day for the rest of her life.

He leaned back and tilted her chin up. "Emma…Emma, what you do to me…"

And then his lips swept down and claimed hers in a kiss.

A kiss that was even better than the one they'd shared in the study.

A kiss that took her breath away.

A kiss that made her heart soar.

She tasted him, tasted the brandy on his lips. Heady. Sensuous. *God in heaven!* She almost swooned when he entwined his tongue with hers.

His lips drifted, tracing the line of her jaw, trailing down her neck, down to the top of her gown—leaving her breathless and wanting more…so much more.

"I will keep you safe, Emma," he murmured in between kisses. "I promise. I promise…" He said it like a mantra. Like a prayer.

She did believe him. She had never doubted his courage. His bravery.

His strength, his powerful arms around her, made her heart pound in her ears.

The scent of him—soap, sandalwood, citrus, leather, and brandy—washed away her lingering panic and fear about Morgrave.

The breath she didn't know she'd been holding shuddered out of her. Suddenly, it wasn't fear that consumed her. It was him.

His lips traveled back to her mouth to capture hers once more.

His kiss was fierce, demanding, as if he needed to prove something to her.

She let herself fall into it, trembling and tasting, kissing him back as fiercely as he was kissing her.

She heard him groan, and she felt a feminine power surge

through her, power that she could make him know as much desire as he made her feel.

She twined her hands in his hair, and he groaned again. His hands moved down her arms and up her back, making her shiver, as she felt the goosebumps along her skin.

He finally broke the kiss and touched his forehead to hers. "If I don't stop now, I won't be able to ever stop…" he rasped.

She leaned back and gazed up at him, dreamily searching his face. "I wish we didn't have to stop… But I understand."

"God, woman. What you do to me!"

"Are you going to be grumpy again?"

"Hell no! But if I don't leave now, I fear for my virtue."

She burst into laughter. "We mustn't have that. If you don't have your virtue, what do you have?"

"Happiness? Satisfaction? I can think of many other things worth having…" He stepped back and blew out a deep breath.

"Thank you for the flowers." She smiled. "And the apology."

"Thank you for forgiving me." He grinned. "And for *un-stinkifying* the salve."

He turned to walk to the door, but before he left, she stood on her tiptoes and kissed him on the cheek. "Goodnight, Michael."

"Goodnight, Emma."

LONG AFTER MICHAEL left, Emma lay in her bed, thinking about their conversation and their kiss. She believed that Michael, Wright, and Armstrong would work with the authorities to capture Morgrave. She hoped it would be soon. But what would happen after? She and Katie would leave and go home. Go back to live with Evie and Martin—wherever they were living once this was all over. But there was one thing that would not be over, and that was her feelings for Michael. Because now she knew that she was in love with him. Completely, and hopelessly in love…

CHAPTER SEVENTEEN

Two days later

EMMA JOLTED AWAKE, realizing she had much to accomplish, yet remained cozily tucked in bed. She had overslept, likely due to the stress of organizing the surprise birthday party. Thankfully, her friends—Stanhope, Hastings, Wright, and Mrs. Peppers—had all been a tremendous help. They all cared about Michael and wanted to do something nice for him. Emma was in full agreement on that front.

They had decided to host the gathering in the "hidden" game room, which, aside from the ballroom, was the largest room and had barely been used in years. It was also the farthest room from the main part of the house, having been a relatively recent addition built at the back of the manor. After a thorough cleaning, tables and chairs were brought in and set up throughout to accommodate the staff, friends, and family who would be attending. It was a miracle that they had managed to keep the preparations a secret from Michael.

Luckily, Celia, Lady Beadle, and even Aunt Chippie had also been helping with the party preparations and spending time with Katie over the past few days. Even the artist, Burns, had stayed on and given Katie sketching and painting lessons. Katie had whispered to Emma that they were creating a grand gift for Michael, in addition to her birthday sign. Meanwhile, Wright and Armstrong had kept Michael engaged in discussing the manhunt they'd set in motion to catch Morgrave.

Emma shivered at the thought that the arsonist was somewhere out there—perhaps even in the area. Michael had hired even more men to guard the property. The stonemason and his workers had almost completed fortifying the wall that surrounded the estate.

She had faith that they would catch the arsonist, now that they knew who he was. Fortunately, she was so busy that whenever her thoughts veered in that direction, she took on yet another task that needed doing before the party. However, keeping herself from thinking about Michael and their kiss the other night was next to impossible. She must have gone over their conversation at least ten times—and the kiss she'd thought about so many times, she'd lost count. But how could she *not* think about it when she'd realized that she was in love with Michael? Nor could she keep herself from thinking about what would happen when Morgrave was caught and the danger had passed.

She and Katie would return to London, for there would no longer be any need for them to impose on Michael's privacy. Celia had extended an invitation for Katie and Emma to stay with them in London, but had been overruled by Lady Beadle, who'd insisted they stay with her as long as they wanted.

Evie and Martin had sent word that they would stay on at Martin's family's estate until after the baby was born. Evie was too close to her due date, and it would be unsafe for her to travel. But eventually they would return to London, and they would all be reunited. Emma looked forward to that day with all her heart. Especially meeting her new niece or nephew. She missed Evie and Martin terribly, and she knew Katie missed them even more.

But what about my feelings for Michael?

Could she tell Michael of her feelings for him? Should she?

That was not a one-sided kiss…

What if Michael was just caught up in the heat of the moment when he apologized and found out who the arsonist was?

But what about the comforting words he'd shared with her, promising to protect her and Katie? Could it all be because they had been spending so much time together? After all, they've been living under the same roof for several weeks now. Emma felt a little confused and unsure about what it all meant.

In the past few days, she had been so very busy, but she couldn't help but wonder if Michael had been purposely avoiding her.

And what am I to make of that?

She heaved a deep sigh as she set aside her swirling thoughts and reached for the list she'd left on her side table of what she still needed to accomplish for the party. Luckily, they'd gotten the bulk of everything prepared. All that was left for her to do was to put the finishing touches on her gift for Michael. She was still counting on Wright keeping Lord Wilton engaged long enough to allow them time to set up the surprise—and finish her gift.

Having decided to make two larger jars of salve, she realized she needed to make haste.

As she was slipping her wrapper on, the door opened, and Doris entered carrying a tray of chocolate and a slice of toast with a small pot of Emma's favorite fruit preserves.

"Good morning, Doris. I'm afraid I slept much later than I planned," Emma said as Doris set the tray down on the bed.

"No trouble at all. You've been so busy these past few days that I didn't want to disturb you, my lady."

"Thank you," Emma said before she took a sip of the delicious chocolate. "Would you mind watching Katie for a couple of hours? I have a few things I need to take care of."

"Certainly, my lady. I enjoy watching Miss Katie and Finn play together in the garden. It's like they've been together since they were wee ones," Doris said, as she laid out a pink muslin dress for Emma. "I also pressed the deep-green muslin dress for you. It's such a pretty frock."

"Katie and I seem to have more dresses than we can possibly wear," Emma said with a smile. "And they are all so beautiful."

"The modiste did a wonderful job," Doris agreed. "My lady, you mustn't try to put your corset on by yourself," she chided, stepping over to Emma. "Please allow me to help you finish dressing."

Emma smiled. "Thank you." She turned to grip the bedpost as Doris expertly laced her corset and adjusted her petticoats. Once they had finished, she bent down to slip on her half boots, preparing for a trip to the stable. Reluctant to ruin the delicate pink satin slippers the modiste had sent along with the dress, she opted for practicality instead. "I still need to finish Michael's gift," she half whispered to herself, the thought of it lingering uppermost in her mind as she got ready.

"It's a mighty important day, Lady Emma," Doris continued, as if she hadn't heard her. The older woman skirted around the bed, hanging up the clothing from the day before and picking up Emma's nightclothes. "Everyone is excited about the birthday party."

"Yes! I know Katie plans to finish her birthday sign well before the party. She told me Mr. Burns has been helping her," Emma said as she opened the door. "If anyone is looking for me, I'll be back in an hour."

"Yes, my lady. Don't worry about Miss Katie. I'll keep an eye on her and Finn," Doris said, before Emma nodded and departed the room.

She scooted out the kitchen door and headed for the stables, intent on getting the salve finished.

"Are you heading to the stables?" Michael asked, appearing from nowhere.

Emma jumped. "Where did *you* come from, Michael? You scared me." *Drat!* Wasn't Wright supposed to be keeping Michael occupied?

"You shouldn't be out here on your own, Emma," he chided softly.

"But you told me the estate was secure," she said, blushing as her eyes met Michael's. *There I go, thinking of that kiss again.*

"Yes, the estate is secure. If anything happens, Armstrong, Wright, and I have established a way of signaling the guards to alert them. They will immediately lock down the grounds."

"Thank you for making us safe," she said softly.

"You're welcome," he said. "In any event, it would be better if you would allow me to escort you, purely for precaution."

Emma drew a deep breath and nodded. She had no choice. She'd have to think of something when they got there. He had already ruined the element of surprise, where the salve was concerned, since he'd discovered her in the back room in the stables a few days ago, blending the scented oils into the salve. Even so, making a salve that he could use was important to her. It was something she wanted to do.

"I'd be happy for you to escort me," she said.

Minutes later, they arrived at the stable, and Michael looked around. "Should I wait here?"

She was relieved she didn't have to ask, and nodded. "I have a few things I wanted to check on and won't be long." *No doubt he's guessed what I'm up to, in any case.*

"I wanted to show you something," he said, turning to point toward something.

Emma followed his gaze and saw a small pond tucked behind the stables, beyond the tall grasses. "Is that a pond?"

Michael smiled. "It is." He took her hand and gently rubbed his thumb in her palm as, together, they walked to the pond.

Having her hand tucked inside of his big, warm one and rubbing her palm made her feel all tingly inside, and she realized she wanted more—she wanted him to kiss her again.

"It's not far, now," he said, still holding her hand as they tromped through ragged, tall grass. Hidden behind the clump of grass was a small pier with a brown, flat-bottom boat tied to a wooden post in the water at the end of the dock. "I think my relative not only liked billiards, but he also enjoyed fishing. I saw this pond from my study when I first arrived, but only this week decided to explore it. And when I did, I discovered this small boat."

"What makes you sure he liked to fish?" she asked.

"I can only assume so. The pond is stocked with fish," he said, grinning. "From your blank expression, I'm going to guess you've never fished."

She shook her head. "I've never been fishing."

"Would you care for a small trip across the pond? And if you decide you'd like to learn to fish, I'd be glad to teach you. I checked the boat, and it's sound. No leaks," Michael said with a crooked smile.

Good Lord! That smile nearly made her swoon. Gazing into his eyes, Emma knew it was exactly what she'd like to do…with him. Good thing she'd gotten the bulk of her duties done yesterday. "Yes. I would enjoy that."

"Good. Shall we?"

"Oh! Yes, but I still have something to attend to in the stables. I won't be long. Can you wait outside?"

"You make it sound mysterious," he said, laughing, as they walked back to the stables. "Very well, I'll wait right here."

"Thank you."

Before releasing her hand, Michael leaned down and pressed a gentle kiss into the center of her palm. "Maybe next time, I can teach you to fish, Emma," he suggested, a playful glint in his eyes.

"I would like that," she replied, her voice barely above a whisper.

With her heart thumping with anticipation, Emma raced back to the stables. She quickly withdrew two jars of salve and two vials of essential oils from her pockets, confident she had calculated the perfect blend of scents, tailored to the size of the jars. As she mixed the recipe, the aromas swirled together in a delightful bouquet that filled the air with warmth and promise.

Once she completed the mixture, a thought struck her. She couldn't very well go fishing with Michael with salve in her pocket. She decided to leave the jars behind, allowing the oils to better settle into the salve before the party. After all, she didn't want Michael glimpsing her gift. Besides the salve, she had polished up the small brass-and-wood penknife. Impulsively, she reached into her pocket and found the small packet containing the knife. It was wrapped in several small handkerchiefs she had made from fabric scraps and embroidered his initials on. At least *that* would be a surprise, she thought.

Before stepping out, she made sure to crack the windows, letting a gentle breeze waft through the stable to prevent the fresh sandalwood and orange aroma from overwhelming the air in the small room. Seeing a small drawer, she tucked the essential oils inside, deciding they would be there when she next needed them.

WHEN HE'D SPIED Emma slipping from the house alone, Michael seized the opportunity to spend some time with her and insisted on escorting her. Not only would he be able to protect her, but this would be the perfect opportunity to show her the pond, he'd thought.

He smiled as he waited for her to return from inside the stable. From her nervous demeanor when they arrived there, he assumed that she was at the stable to work on masking his salve and offered to wait outside. After Michael had complimented her on her work on the ointment, Hastings had used it several times and was down to the dregs of the experimental jar she had created. Hopefully he wasn't being presumptuous, because the salve was working on his leg, and he sincerely hoped she was making some more.

As she emerged from the stables, Michael felt a rush of admiration sweep over him. Her red hair danced in the wind, cascading behind her like a fiery waterfall. He caught his breath, captivated by her beauty. Today, he was excited to spend time with her at the pond, a dream he had nurtured since he'd spotted the rowboat drydocked at the end of a small, almost-hidden pier.

The pond was secluded enough that he hoped to even find a moment to kiss her.

"We might have enough time for a quick boat ride," he said, glancing up at the dark patches of clouds that had formed above them seemingly out of nowhere.

"I would enjoy that," Emma said, a grin lighting up her face. "I don't swim, so I'm going to take you at your word that there are no leaks in the boat."

"Ha! Rest assured. The pond is stocked with fish and possibly turtles. I have no wish to return with both of us dripping wet. Imagine how we'd try to explain that to dear Aunt Chippie and Lady Beadle."

Emma laughed. "Indeed! That's an excellent point, *my lord.*" Her voice was teasing. "And I trust completely that we won't find ourselves capsizing."

Michael had barely had time to speak with her over the past few days, given how busy he'd been securing the property with Wright and Armstrong, and the work being done by the stonemason and his men.

But he'd *wanted* to spend time with her, and he'd sought her out that morning, hoping to show her the pond and take her out on the boat. It was a peaceful place, and he'd wanted to speak to her. The kiss they'd shared the other night was etched in his mind. But he couldn't just keep kissing her. He couldn't just keep taking advantage of her. Not when he had such deep feelings for her.

He'd sworn he'd never marry, especially with this injury he'd obtained in France. But he had begun to realize that maybe there was that one special woman for him—one who would accept him with his flaws. Someone that he could love. He now realized that he wanted the type of marriage that centered around love and respect. Emma *mattered* to him, but he had begun to realize his feelings for her were much more than simply *mattering*. He had begun to feel what could only be described as love.

Over drinks one night, he'd asked Armstrong how he'd

known Celia was the one for him. "It's when she's all you think about, and you can't imagine existing without her," Armstrong had replied.

The words had remained with Michael. He realized that was how he had begun to feel about Emma. But it was only a matter of time before Emma left his home and returned to London to be with her family. If he wanted to have a chance with her, he needed to share his feelings—soon.

It was also becoming painfully obvious to him that she was intent on doing things her way, even when he'd asked her not to go outside alone.

As he rowed the small boat out to the center of the pond, Michael felt the first drop of rain. "Emma, I don't think today is meant for our boat ride. And if I'm to keep my promise of not having us return to the house looking like drowned rats, we should head back. Those clouds look serious."

"I believe you are right," she said, gazing at him. "Maybe next time we can talk about that fishing lesson."

He rowed the two of them back and moored the boat as he found it, safely secured to the pier. As they neared the stables, he leaned down, hoping for a kiss, but was interrupted by Katie calling for Emma and Finn barking excitedly.

"I suppose she's been looking for me. We should hurry back," Emma said.

"Sounds like Finn may have found a rabbit," he said, laughing.

"Well, I hope he leaves the poor thing alone," Emma said. "I don't think I'd like to explain to Katie what happens to the bunny if he catches it."

Michael would have sworn there was a sincere look of disappointment on her face when he pulled back from his intended kiss, which sent a jolt of joy to his heart. He was suddenly determined that he'd find another chance to kiss her.

FROM A CONCEALED vantage point behind the weathered stone wall, where he was certain he couldn't be seen, Morgrave adjusted his spyglass. His heart raced as he reassured himself that no one could detect his presence. "I see her," he whispered. "I knew it! She's here. Soon, you will be mine, my beautiful redhead," he mused, captivated by her allure. "My plan worked."

A quiet hiss escaped him as he carefully watched the man and woman he had been stalking. Adjusting his lens for a sharper view, he suddenly felt a surge of fury as he saw Wilton kiss her palm. "He has no right to touch her and will regret it. She belongs to me…and I will make her mine in every way, very soon."

Tucking the spyglass securely in his pocket, Morgrave took out a flask and took a long, heavy swig. Impatience gnawed at him; he was tired of waiting to have her. Soon, he would put the final touches of his plan into motion and make Wilton regret ever taking the flame-haired beauty from him.

CHAPTER EIGHTEEN

"*S*URPRISE!"

As he entered the gaming room, the curtains were dramatically pulled back and a burst of sunshine flooded the space, revealing the large group of well-wishers standing in a large semicircle.

Michael stood still, stunned as his gaze took in the jubilant gathering of friends and family. Their eager faces sparkled with anticipation, especially the small girl bouncing on her toes, eyes wide with excitement, and the red-and-white spaniel happily wagging his tail beside her. Standing behind them with her hands on the little girl's shoulders was the woman who'd completely upended his life since the moment he laid eyes on her. Above them, a sign crafted in blue and red letters in a child's scrawl read, *Happy Birthday*.

"Woof, woof!"

Realizing his mouth hung open and he was staring, Michael closed it and looked to his two friends who had entered the room with him. "Wright, Armstrong... Are either of *you* celebrating a birthday today?" he quipped, his brow arched even as he felt his face flush at all the attention.

"No, not me. Are you, Wright?" Armstrong said, his expression neutral.

"Um. I suppose, looking at the spread of treats and food on

the table, I should claim it, but my birthday's still several months off. Could it be *yours*, Michael?" Wright asked innocently.

"It's your birthday, Lord Michael!" Katie shouted with a happy squeal of delight, clapping her hands. "We fooled him, Auntie!"

"*Woof! Woof!*" Finn barked.

Michael looked at Emma. Her glowing smile nearly took his breath away. She was wearing a blue muslin gown that made her violet eyes shimmer, and her lush hair was up in a simple style that only enhanced her beauty. "You did all of this for me?" He took in everyone, realizing Emma couldn't have done this without help. "All of you? You did this?"

Cheers and well-wishes echoed from the group.

"I don't know what to say," he said.

"Say thank you and let's get on with it," Wright said. "Just looking at all this food has my mouth watering—oh, are those deviled eggs, Mrs. Pepper?"

The short, rotund woman smiled, her eyes twinkling with mischief as she nodded knowingly. "Ah, your favorite, I see. But patience is a virtue, dear Lord Wright; you'll have to wait a little longer before indulging."

Michael laughed at the cook's deft handling of his best friend. Wright was known for indulging in a few favorite foods when he visited, and Michael suspected he'd had a hand in getting his cook to make deviled eggs—admittedly, a tasty treat. "Thank you…all of you. This is a surprise…a wonderful surprise," he said, his voice husky with emotion. He was moved by the efforts they had gone to in planning this surprise. Hell, he'd even forgotten it *was* his birthday.

"Can we cut the cake?" Katie asked. "Oops, I forgot." She looked up at her aunt, who looked at Wright.

Wright smiled and plucked glasses of champagne from a footman's tray for Michael, Armstrong, and himself. Other footmen had circulated champagne among the rest of the guests gathered in the room, while Katie was given a glass of lemonade.

Lifting his glass high, Wright launched into a toast:

"Happy birthday, my dear friend.
May good health and everyday cheer,
Be with you every day and every year.
May fortune smile upon you with every new day.
And blessings surround you, whether you're blond or gray!"

"Where did that blessing come from?" Armstrong teased. "Especially the last line."

"Just another one of my many talents," Wright said, flashing a sly smile. "I've been known to craft a poetic line or two. I'm not just a pretty face, you know."

"Do you like your surprise, Lord Michael?" Katie said, hopping up and down with excitement.

Michael crouched down, barely wincing, thanks to the salve that Hastings had been massaging into his leg over the past few days. "I loved it," Michael said, kissing the top of Katie's head and scratching Finn behind the ears.

"Finn was really good at keeping the secret, weren't you, Finn?" Katie said, patting the dog's head.

Finn gave a woof of agreement.

"Indeed," Michael said as he picked up the little girl. "You were all very good at keeping the secret." His eyes met Emma's, and he winked at her, enjoying the pretty blush that tinted her cheeks.

"Did you see my sign?" Katie asked, pointing up.

"I did, Katie," he said, chuckling. The sign was so big it would be visible from the other side of the estate. "It's truly a masterpiece. I'd love to leave it hanging here for a while, if that's all right with you."

She hugged him. "It's a present for you. Well, one of the presents."

Michael hugged the little girl back. "Thank you, Katie. I will cherish it."

"Come, Katie, let's get you something to eat," Doris said, taking the girl off his hands.

"What is your most favorite gift that you've ever received?" Emma asked him cheekily.

"Ooh…that's a hard one. Perhaps I've yet to receive it and will get it later tonight," Michael quipped, waggling his eyebrows. He looked around, hoping they could find an excuse to leave for a few moments so he could steal a kiss.

"Happy birthday, Michael," Lady Beadle and Aunt Chippie called out from the other side of the room as they approached him.

Masking a sigh with a forced smile, he winked at Emma, knowing that he'd have to wait longer for that kiss. "Maybe when the party is over," he whispered, keeping an eye on the two older women who were weaving their way from the other side of the room. "There's something I want to speak with you about."

"Of course," Emma said, sounding breathless. She looked up in the direction of approaching pair. "I should check on Katie." She left to do so.

"Wilton," Armstrong said, walking up to him, "I believe we were correct in our assessment that the fire at Lady Beadle's was deliberately set. I received word from London that the man depicted in Burns's drawing was recognized by several of Lady Beadle's neighbors as the fellow watching from across the street when the carriage house burned. And Headquarters has put out an alert out for Lord Morgrave, but no one has seen him yet."

Michael cleared his throat. "Should we discuss this in my study?"

Armstrong nodded, though he appeared troubled. He mouthed an apology to both Michael and Wright, indicating they could discuss it later.

Nearby, Aunt Chippie gasped softly. "My gosh, Millie! Did I hear that right? Someone set your house on fire?" she said kindly, her voice filled with concern and compassion. "I had no idea." She gently approached her old friend and gave her a comforting hug.

"Yes, Peg, they did," Lady Beadle said. "I fear it might be the same criminal who set poor Emma and Katie's house on fire. He put a torch to my carriage house. Luckily, my footman and ostler saw the flames and were able to contain them and douse them without any of our animals being injured in the process. So, I decided to check on Emma and Katie."

"I'm sorry that your house was damaged, dear Millie," Aunt Chippie said, gasping softly. "How awful. I even heard an older couple died in a recent fire that was set deliberately."

"Yes! Dreadful circumstances. Emma and Katie came to me after the fire at Emma's brother-in-law's and sister's home, riding Katie's parents' horses. They saw the man." Lady Beadle visibly shivered and wiped a tear from her face. "The sooner we can find that dreadful man, the better."

"Ladies, I must thank you for this wonderful party," Michael said, hoping to change the discussion, moving it away from the discussion of Morgrave. His men were outside, helping to ensure everyone's safety.

"I must say, this is a fabulous birthday party—and just the perfect size. I prefer parties that provide a chance to speak with every guest," Lady Beadle said.

From the corner of his eye, Michael saw Emma say something to Wright, who winked at her before she quietly left the room. A strange wave of jealousy swept over him, making him pause for a moment. Were they planning some sort of liaison? As ridiculous as that seemed, even to him, Michael couldn't seem to help himself. He wasn't even sure he had the right to be jealous. There had been no promises between them. There had barely even been any kisses.

Suddenly, he felt an overwhelming need to remedy that.

But before he could take a step, Burns stepped forward and handed him a large, flat, rectangular package. "It's a sketch that I think you'll enjoy. And if you come to Brighton, I'll be glad to paint it for you."

"Thank you, Mr. Burns. Shall I open it now?" Michael asked,

suddenly getting the feeling that the artist might want him to wait.

"I think perhaps you'll want to open it when Lady Emma and Miss Katie are with you," Burns replied, smiling. "Besides, it's a pencil drawing, and sometimes the soft lead tends to smear. Perhaps it needs a bit more time to dry. I rushed it."

"I imagine you will be very pleased, Lord Wilton," Aunt Chippie said. "But I do agree with Mr. Burns. Sometimes a surprise is even more wonderful when we wait."

"That's true, Aunt Chippie," Wright said, biting back a smile that looked more like a smirk to Michael.

Wright's smirk irritated Michael. Did he know something about the sketch? Maybe he'd ask when they were alone. He felt another surge of jealousy. First, he'd seen Wright whispering with Emma, their heads close together, and now he had to contend with his friend knowing something about Emma that he didn't.

"Pish-posh," said Lady Beadle. "Honestly, Chippie, you've never waited in your life for anything."

"I thought you two had mended fences?" Wright quipped.

"Well, we have, mostly. But what's the fun in that, eh, Chippie?"

"Quite right, dear Millie," Aunt Chippie said with a smirk. "Your penchant for snide remarks is unparalleled."

Much to Michael's relief, Mrs. Peppers stepped forward in the nick of time. "My lord, I made your favorite vanilla-strawberry angel food cake, but if we don't cut into it, I'm afraid Miss Katie will be most upset." Michael smiled as his gaze landed on Katie, who was seated next to Celia on a nearby settee, playing some sort of pretend game with her doll. "Besides, I'm looking at some hungry people here."

Everyone burst into laughter.

"Then please do the honors, Mrs. Peppers," Michael said.

As Mrs. Peppers nodded and hurried off to cut the cake, Michael thanked everyone again, singling out Hastings, who, back in their battlefield days, had always made sure to mark his birthday, organizing a small gathering with their fellow soldiers. Even in the intervening years when Michael would have preferred to forget, his friend always reminded him that life was worth celebrating. Ironically, given all that had been going on, he'd forgotten he'd already told Hastings not to make a fuss this year.

"Hastings, I appreciate the effort that must have gone into planning this party. Thank you," Michael said.

"I can't take the credit, my lord," his valet replied. "It was Lady Emma's idea. She organized the entire event. We were merely her helpers. She insisted that you should celebrate surrounded by family and friends."

Michael felt a rush of warmth in his heart at learning the party was Emma's idea. Just one more reason why he couldn't wait to speak to her. Alone.

Well, the talking part would happen after the kissing part.

"Ah, then a special thank you to Lady Emma…" Michael said with a smile, glancing around. "Has anyone seen Lady Emma?" Confound it, where *was* she?

"She said she needed to go to the stables to retrieve something for you in there—a present," Wright said. "But to be honest, that was quite some time ago."

A cold jolt of dread suddenly coursed through Michael. Something was wrong. Something was *very* wrong. "Wright, come with me. I might be overreacting, but…"

"I don't think you're overreacting," Wright said grimly as he signaled Armstrong. "Come to think of it, I don't see Finn anywhere either, and he's usually attached to Katie."

"Keep an eye on things," Michael said to Hastings in a low voice. "Especially Katie."

Hastings nodded. "I will, my lord."

Michael turned and made his way out, along with Armstrong and Wright. The three men broke into a run after they exited the billiard room.

He prayed that he was wrong and that his worst fears had not come true.

⟫⟫⟩⟨⟨⟨

EMMA WAS IRRITATED that she'd forgotten the salve. She didn't want to miss one moment of the party. She couldn't wait to give Michael his gift, albeit not a surprise gift, considering he already knew she'd been able to mask the atrocious smell a few days ago, when he caught her doing just that in the back room in the stables.

Had it only been a few days? It felt like a lifetime ago when he'd lashed out at her after finding her mixing the salve just days before. She'd been hurt and angry at first, but when he came to see her with a bunch of flowers and apologized and shared with her his deepest vulnerability, her heart had melted. Michael was so strong and courageous in so many ways—to her, he'd always seemed invincible. To find out that he carried more than just physical scars from the war had touched her soul. That he trusted her enough to tell her meant the world to her. And then he'd kissed her—and it was even better than the one they'd shared in the study.

She could no longer deny her feelings for him. The question was, did he feel the same? She thought he felt something for her. When he'd taken her out on the pond, onto the boat earlier that day it was almost as though he were courting her, and then at the party, the way he looked at her made her knees nearly buckle.

She didn't know what the future held for them, but she hoped she could work up the courage to find out.

Until they found and arrested the arsonist, their lives would continue to be up in limbo—but tonight...tonight was about Michael and celebrating his birthday.

"I can't wait for him to open his other gifts," she said aloud, patting the wrapped penknife in the pocket of her gown. "How about you, Finn?" The dog had decided to come with her, happily trotting next to her and wagging his tail.

Emma had embroidered a set of handkerchiefs from rem-

156

nants that the modiste had given her and had wrapped them with the ornately carved penknife she'd found in the attic. After she'd cleaned and polished it, she knew Michael would love it.

"Woof!" the spaniel said as they rounded the corner to the stable entrance. They made their way to the room at the back, where she'd left the jars of salve. Opening the drawer of the worktable, she was relieved to see the two jars were still where she had left them. Hastings had shrewdly suggested she make two, given that he was now massaging Michael's leg twice a day, morning and night, and they'd already seen a significant difference.

Finn barked and began to sniff around the room.

"What you're smelling is the salve, Finn," Emma pointed out. She opened a jar and let him smell it. But the dog didn't seem convinced.

"Woof," he barked, this time turning toward the door and giving a guttural growl.

"Finn, what are you growling about? Is it a fox or an owl?" Emma said, suddenly wishing she had asked Michael to come out here so that she could give him his gift in private. They could have come out here together, and maybe this time, he would have kissed her in the stable. But who knows? Maybe she would have been the daring one to kiss him!

Finn growled again, making the hair at the back of her neck stand up. She didn't know what sort of animal was out there, but whatever it was, it was clearly making Finn on edge. She knew that Michael had hired additional men to guard the property. So why did she feel like something was wrong? A shiver crept up her spine as she slipped the jars into her pockets. "Come on, Finn. Let's head back to the party and enjoy ourselves."

As she stepped from the small room, a large hand clamped over her mouth, followed by a low, raspy laugh. Emma's heart leaped to her throat as her worst fear came true. But she wouldn't go down without a fight. She bit the hand, as hard as she could, and heard a grunt. Then she felt the back of his hand slap her across the face, making her stumble back.

"You're a fiery bitch, aren't you? Good, I like that."

"Get away from me, you fiend," she said, trembling with fear and rage. "You're not going to get away with this."

"And what makes you say that?"

"Because everyone knows who you are…*Viscount Morgrave!*"

His eyes flashed with fury. "It doesn't matter now, because soon, I'll be long gone. With you by my side."

Finn growled once more and ran in front of her. "Good boy, Finn," she sobbed as she grabbed on to a wooden post and pulled herself up.

"Do you think that mongrel can save you?"

Finn replied for her with a low, menacing bark.

"He has more courage than you do!" she said defiantly.

"We'll see about that!" Morgrave said as he lunged at her, spinning her around and pushing her up against the wooden post.

Finn leaped at Morgrave, his teeth latching on to his leg. Morgrave hissed as he shook off the dog. Finn yelped as he landed hard on the hard-packed earth of the stables.

"Don't hurt him!" Emma cried out.

"If he behaves, I might let him live," Morgrave said as he stuffed a foul-tasting rag into her mouth. Jerking her hands behind her back, he tied her wrists together with a rough length of rope. "You're mine now, firewoman," he rasped in her ear.

Suddenly, a burlap sack was thrown over her head, tightening as Morgrave secured it. He hoisted her over his shoulder, rendering her somewhat helpless.

Desperate to escape, and with only her feet free, she kicked as hard as she could, but she began to feel a darkness encroach on her, and it wasn't just the bag over her head… It was something else, something that was making it hard for her to move and think. And then she realized, the foul-tasting gag…it must have been laudanum. She needed to warn Michael…but how?

Somewhere close by, she heard Finn valiantly defending her against the intruder. She could hear a struggle—the sound of her brave companion fighting back. But then she heard a guttural curse followed by a sickening thud and a whimper.

"Flea-bitten beast! That'll teach you!"

Emma's heart sank as she realized the depth of her peril. *Oh, God, Finn… I have to fight…have to fight…have to…*

But the darkness was too much, pulling her under until everything went black.

CHAPTER NINETEEN

"THAT SOUNDS LIKE Finn," Michael said at the sound of distant barking and whining. But he knew the sound of Finn's barks, and this sounded like the dog had been hurt.

Something was very wrong.

"That bastard is here!"

The three men raced through the kitchen to the back door, the quickest way to the stables. Michael threw open the door to find Finn lying on the bottom step to the entryway, shaking and bleeding.

The dog held up his head as he managed to stand. His fur was stained with blood from what looked to be a large, deep gash on his side.

Michael carefully picked up the trembling dog, who was whimpering in pain. "He's been severely kicked," Michael said, as a cold dread shot up his spine. "It's all right, my brave lad—we'll get you fixed in no time." The dog covered his face with licks.

"It's Morgrave," he said in a grim tone. "He's here and he has her." The words tasted bitter on his tongue. His heart plummeted. This was his fault. He had promised to keep Emma safe, and he'd failed her.

Wright pulled a whistle out of his pocket and sharply blew three times, the agreed-upon emergency signal to the guards manning the estate that the perimeter had been breached. The guards would know to come to the house immediately for directions.

"I can take Finn back in, and then I'll join you," Armstrong said, taking the dog in his arms and turning just as the door swung open. Hastings and Stanhope both rushed out and stopped in their tracks.

"My lord?" Hastings asked.

"Lady Emma has been taken," Michael said. "It appears Finn tried to defend her but was hurt. Hastings, I remember seeing Dr. Bianchi at the party talking to Lady Beadle. Take Finn inside and ask Dr. Bianchi to help him."

"I'll take care of him, my lord." Carefully, Hastings took the dog from Armstrong and quickly carried him inside the house.

"Let's go," Michael said.

They began to run toward the stables when they saw the smoke billowing up. "Look!" Wright shouted.

"My God, the bastard set fire to the stables," Armstrong bit out.

"I'll organize the fire brigade," Stanhope said, out of breath, as he arrived behind the men.

"Stanhope, I'd rather you go back inside—you've been through enough in your life." Michael didn't want his loyal retainer to get hurt.

"Never you mind about that, my lord," Stanhope countered. "Look lively, boys," he shouted to the footmen who'd been on patrol and had just arrived.

"We'll put the horses in the corral," Michael said as they all rushed into the stables.

Within minutes, Michael, Wright, and Armstrong, along with several footmen, got the horses out, locking them into the outer ring, away from the burning structure.

As Michael and the others rescued the horses, Stanhope and the other footmen were joined by Mrs. Peppers and several servants from the house, along with Burns and Hastings, who'd no doubt alerted them and left Finn in the care of the doctor.

They'd swiftly formed two lines from the well to the stables and begun putting out the fire.

Stanhope barked out orders to several footmen to douse the hay bales that hadn't yet caught fire to keep it contained.

"Stanhope will have the stables under control," Armstrong said as they corralled the last of the horses.

"We need to find her," Michael said, his voice cracking. He directed his footmen who were the fastest riders to saddle up. "Lord Morgrave—the man in the picture we showed you—has taken Lady Emma Grantham. We need to find them. We'll divide up and search the property. They can't have gotten far," he said as he finished cinching the saddle on his stallion.

"Remember, he's not working alone," Armstrong reminded them. In his initial briefing to Michael and Wright when he first arrived, Armstrong had filled them in on the details of the investigation. "The most recent victims described a plain black carriage that sat outside their house before it was torched. And recall that when I saw him at the inn, my spy outside also noted a plain black carriage."

"I doubt he could have gotten far even with help," Wright said. "You had four men stationed at the gated entrance, and ten men along the wall that faced the main road. They would have seen something and signaled us by now."

"Which is why I think he's still somewhere on the property," Michael said. "We need to search every damn building."

"How many buildings are on the estate, besides the manor house and stable?" Armstrong asked.

"There are several, although I haven't had a chance to investigate them. There's a gamekeeper's cabin, several greenhouses, and a small gardener's shack," Michael said as they mounted up. He clenched his teeth as he climbed into the saddle, pushing away the pain. "We'll split up. We'll each take three guards and check the woods and the vacant buildings. If you find anything, signal," he added.

If anything happened to Emma, he would never forgive himself. She'd been working on that salve for him—he was certain of it. She must have made more for his birthday and had forgotten it in that room in the stables. *Damn it!*

My God! What if she's dead? Michael chilled at the thought. *She can't be dead. I won't let her be.*

"I know you're imagining all sorts of things that could have happened to Emma," Armstrong said, as though reading his mind. "But keep in mind how strong and courageous she is. She went into a burning house and secured what she needed, then gathered two horses from the stable and delivered her niece to safety."

Michael nodded as they rode off. He knew Emma was the bravest woman he'd ever met, but he also knew that Morgrave was a madman.

Please, God, keep her safe!

EMMA'S HEAD THROBBED, and she had rope burns around her ankles and wrists, a stark reminder of her captivity. Confusion clouded her thoughts as she pondered what substance the man had used to render her unconscious. A fog enveloped her mind making it difficult to think. Adding to her distress, she found herself sitting on a dusty, foul-smelling mattress, teeming with bugs of some type—and Lord knew what else, given how itchy her skin was. Her eyes stung, no doubt from the dust, and she felt something crawling on her leg, beneath her skirt, which sent shivers down her spine. Unfortunately, her hands and feet were bound, preventing her from investigating the source of her discomfort. And she dared not shift or move, lest she attract Morgrave's attention.

She closed her eyes, trying to calm her breathing, trying to keep from panicking. Her thoughts drifted to Michael, who had shown her the pond and held her hand, softly rubbing her palm with his thumb. When he pointed out the small, flat-bottomed boat, he'd mentioned teaching her to fish. She wasn't certain she really wanted to learn, but the idea of spending time with Michael on a boat, on a sunny day, sounded wonderful. She could remember his scent as though he were right there beside her: leather, sandalwood, and soap.

Somehow, she had to make it out of here alive. If she did, she would tell him. Tell him how she felt. Even if his feelings weren't the same as hers, she didn't care. She just wanted him to know how much she loved him. How much she cared about him. And how she wanted him to live a happy and full life, even if it wouldn't be with her. She wanted him to be happy.

She needed to keep her wits about her. If she wanted to escape, she had to stay aware of her surroundings. She still felt the dizzying influence of the laudanum, and her eyes itched from the dust. Hoping she could clear them, she squeezed them shut, hoping that the tears forming would somehow wash away some of the dust, providing a little relief. Then she looked about the room, peering into the darkness, trying to see if there was something she could use to untie herself, or as a weapon of some sort.

A door slammed open somewhere nearby, and she heard a heated argument taking place in another room. One voice was cold and mean—it sounded like it belonged to Morgrave. It was a voice she would never forget, for it sounded like the very devil himself. Pushing up against the wall, she put her ear to it and tried to listen.

"Simms, it's about time you showed yourself. Did you get the carriage through?" Morgrave rasped.

"It wasn't easy, but I managed to find a place for it," the man apparently named Simms replied. "It's parked nearby, behind the wall, beneath a grove of trees. As you can see, I unhitched the horses and brought them. It will make it easier. This place is heavily guarded, but I managed to locate a spot where the guards were fewer and slipped in through there. The stone wall almost encircles the whole property. They added several feet of height to it. However, the horses don't have saddles. I didn't have time to find two, so we'll have to ride bareback."

"You were supposed to steal them from the stable," Morgrave yelled, slamming down his fist onto a hard surface. "Can't you do *anything* right?"

"It stayed busy around the stable—you caused quite a stir when you took her and set the stable on fire," Simms said in a low, steady voice. "Did you think I was going to be able to snatch the saddles from the flames? I don't know what dark mischief you are up to this time, but I don't plan to pay the price for your evil." Simms' voice sounded low and steady, as if he was masking fear. She prayed his bravery would hold.

"Is that right?" Morgrave said, his voice dripping with sarcasm. "You'll do as I say, or your pretty wife and daughter will bear the consequences."

Emma heard a chair slam to the ground, followed by a scuffle.

"Don't threaten my family again, Morgrave," Simms said.

"Or…what?" Morgrave demanded, his voice menacing.

Simms said nothing for a moment. "Are you ready to go to the carriage?" he asked.

"Yes," Morgrave said.

"Did you decide *where* you are going?" Simms asked.

"I thought about taking the boat in Brighton to Portugal but have decided to go to Scotland instead. My mother's family has plenty of property. As the grandson of a Scottish laird—who still lives—I can step into that role and will be protected by my clan. The Scots are a hearty lot. And I can marry her as soon as we cross into Scotland, so no one can kiss my woman again." Morgrave laughed maniacally.

"Lord Morgrave, we should leave now. There are guards on foot and horseback all around, so the sooner we leave here, the better."

"Perhaps Lord Wilton didn't get his money's worth—and our presence here proves that," Morgrave said. "I had no trouble getting inside the estate and finding her. I only needed to wait for the right moment to snatch her. Speaking of my fire princess, I'll get her, and we can leave. She was still unconscious from the laudanum when you arrived. It will be better for her if she stays that way until we cross the border. I have plans for my beautiful fire princess—once I marry her and make her mine."

My God! What is he talking about? Emma gasped, startled by what she'd just overheard. *Marriage? Scotland?* And he'd set fire to the stables. She prayed no one was hurt, and that they'd found Finn before the fire spread.

She tried to stop herself from trembling as she heard his boots approaching.

The bastard was right about one thing. Being asleep, or rather, pretending to be asleep, would hopefully give her the element of surprise as she tried to think of a plan of escape. Feeling in her pocket, she suddenly recalled Michael's gift, wrapped in handkerchiefs. She could use it to cut the rope on her hands. Hastily, she tugged on the string and unwrapped it, shoving the handkerchiefs in one pocket. With her hand on the penknife, she sliced through the ropes around her hands and tossed them beneath the bed. Then, quickly, she tucked the knife in her pocket and settled back into her previous position, closing her eyes and trying to calm her panic. Once her head cleared, she hoped she would find an opportunity to use the knife to help her escape.

The door opened, and candlelight washed over her, but Emma focused on keeping her eyes closed and her breathing even.

"There you are, my fire princess. Even sleeping on this dirty, dingy cot, you glow with fiery beauty. Ah…my dear, I've wanted you since the moment I saw you, outside your house. I let you escape that night, thinking I could easily snatch you whenever I chose. But you proved to be more of a challenge to me. But I have never backed down from a challenge. Especially when it comes to you, my beauty," he said, tucking a lock of her hair behind her ears. "Hmm…your hair is even more beautiful up close. The color of the flames I love so much. Sleep, my fire princess, for when we reach Scotland, I shall awaken you with a kiss and then make you mine forever," he rasped with a low laugh that sent chills coursing up her spine.

How am I going to get away from this madman?

She prayed that Michael would find her in time.

Please, Michael. Please hurry.

CHAPTER TWENTY

Early Evening

"WE'VE CHECKED EVERY damn outbuilding on the property. And we scoured almost every inch of the forested area," Michael said grimly to Armstrong and Wright, who'd met up with him in a clearing in the densely wooded area bordering the western side of the estate.

They'd ordered the other footmen to get to the main road and ride ahead in case Morgrave's endgame was Scotland. Where else would he escape to? By now, he likely knew there was a bounty on his head in England. But he'd apparently lived for many years in Scotland, and it was where he, no doubt, still had property and resources. They would need to do all they could to stop that from happening. Once he crossed into Scotland, he could easily force Emma to wed him and then disappear. Michael refused to let that happen.

"I still think they're in these woods," Wright said. "Recall, the fire in the stables hadn't gotten out of control, so it couldn't have been that long from when he set the fire to when we discovered it. And he was on foot, since we didn't see any horse tracks leading away from the stables when we arrived."

"And you already had men stationed at the gated entrance and along the main road," Armstrong added. "The only likely way they could have gotten onto the property is at the very other end of the wooded area where that back road circles behind the estate."

"The stonemason and his workers were just getting to this area," Michael said, raking his hands through his hair. "We'd discussed building a wall there because there was none, and I knew we were vulnerable along that back road. Dammit! This is all my fault. I should have kept a closer eye on her…

"Let's get going—we still have to check the gamekeeper's cottage, and it's almost at the edge of the tree line where that back road is," he growled as he turned his horse in the direction of the cottage.

A few minutes later, Michael spied several broken branches as the three men approached a copse of trees. As they got closer, they saw clear proof that Morgrave had taken Emma this way. Thank goodness they could make out the hoofprints in the soil. As far as he could tell, it appeared that two horses had traveled through here. Leaning forward and ducking under jagged, low-hanging tree limbs, he tightened his jaw at seeing a scrap of blue fabric hanging from a branch. Pulling it off, he recognized it as the same fabric of the gown Emma was wearing at the party. He urged his mount to gallop ahead.

When they got to the gamekeeper's cottage, Michael leaped from his horse, disregarding the sharp jolt of pain to his leg. Slamming open the door, he rushed inside, with Armstrong and Wright on his heels.

"They *were* here," Michael said. "Not very long ago, by the looks of it."

The mattress in the small bedroom was still warm. Was Emma unconscious? Had Morgrave drugged her? Or, God forbid, beaten or raped her?

Spying a piece of cloth stuck between the mattress and the frame of the cot, he tugged it out and saw that it was a man's handkerchief monogrammed with his initials in delicate stitching. He realized Emma had to have made it for him as part of his birthday gift. She must have had it in the pocket of her gown when that bastard kidnapped her.

He showed Armstrong and Wright the handkerchief. "She left it here as a sign to us."

"A sign that she is all right. She's a strong woman, your Emma," Armstrong said, gripping Michael's shoulder.

Michael nodded as he tucked the handkerchief into the pocket of his trousers. Armstrong had said, "Your Emma." When had she become *his*? Had it been after that first heady kiss that night in the study, or after he'd gone to apologize to her with a bunch of flowers, after he'd bitten her head off in the stables? Or had it been long before that?

All he knew was that she had become a part of his life, and he didn't want to lose her. He *couldn't* lose her. Not now. Not ever.

"Look at this," Wright said, holding out another scrap of material. This one was of rough cloth, and it still bore the scent of laudanum.

"Morgrave drugged her!" Michael said between clenched teeth.

"If he's given her laudanum or something similar, it may have slowed them down," Armstrong said.

"Agreed," Wright said. "There are only two sets of hoofprints out there, and one of the horses is weighed down and clearly moving more slowly than the other. One set of prints is shallower, the other has a shorter stride, and the rear tracks are deeper, as if there's more weight."

Michael didn't want to think about that, about Emma being drugged, unconscious, or hurt, with that bastard's filthy hands on her… He couldn't allow his thoughts to go down that dark road. It would only drive him mad. They would find her. They had to.

"Let's get out of here," he said, already striding toward the door. "They're likely headed to the back road, but they can't be that far ahead." He climbed back on his horse and took off as fast as he could through the trees, ignoring the slap of the branches stinging his arms and chest.

The trail they followed dipped down into a small creek bed, and he noticed the tracks from the horses turned east, where they had come from, instead of west, which led to the back road. The tracks then faded out, clearly having been brushed away with several branches, in a hasty attempt to throw any pursuers off track. But rain two days ago had kept the shaded area moist, and the recent dryness helped cast the hoofprints, providing a perfect path for Michael and his men to follow.

Michael was riding as fast as he could. He was in the lead, with Armstrong and Wright following close behind. A heaviness had settled into his chest, and it wasn't due to how fast they were riding, but from the fear that had taken hold. As though a cold, gnarled hand gripped his heart.

Please, Emma... Please stay strong... Please don't lose hope...

Their search had been difficult thus far, given the dense growth of trees and heavy cloud cover, but suddenly there was a shift in the air and the thick clouds drifted away, allowing the moonlight to flood the path ahead.

"I see them!" Michael shouted as the shaft of light hit two figures in the distance. Two horses—a single rider who rode ahead, and the second animal carried a rider and a slender figure in a slumped position. His gut tightened as recognition hit. *Emma!* The bastard had her tied across the horse's rump. One of her arms hung loose, and her head lolled against the horse's thick black coat.

Withdrawing his pistol from his belt, Michael urged his horse to go faster. He was too far behind to get a clean shot—he didn't want to risk hitting Emma.

Morgrave must have sensed they were on their tail, because he glanced over his shoulder and his eyes widened, prompting him to shout something to the rider ahead.

Michael leaned low, his heart thudding in tandem with his stallion's hooves.

I'm coming, Emma...

The branches seemed to claw at him, yet Michael kept moving forward. He could hear Armstrong and Wright following close behind, the hooves of their horses thrumming like drumbeats. They were approaching a thicker stand of trees, and beyond that, he could see the back road that bordered the property. They had to catch up before the criminals reached the road. From there, there were several side roads they could take, and then the pursuers would have to split up. And what if Morgrave had hired his own men to ambush them, thus enabling his escape?

Suddenly, a muffled cry reached Michael's ears as he thundered through the trees. He'd thought she was unconscious, but he saw Emma lift her head slightly, her eyes glazed with pain yet alert. Their gazes met for a fleeting moment, and he saw a glimmer of hope flash in her eyes, sparking a fresh sense of urgency within him as his horse began to gain on the villains.

"Stop, Morgrave!" Michael shouted, his voice cutting through the air. "You won't get away with this!"

Morgrave spun around again, his eyes wide and wild, his face pale. "You won't have her," he yelled. His horse bucked in protest, causing Emma to slip, and Morgrave to slow down. He reached out, grabbing Emma by the hair and yanking her back.

Michael's heart leaped into his throat as he feared she might tumble off the horse and break her neck.

"I'll kill you, Morgrave," Michael growled as he urged his horse faster.

"Simms!" Morgrave yelled at the other rider, who'd slowed down, reaching out to steady Emma to keep her from falling off the horse. "You simpleton! "We'll ride ahead, and you shoot at them to slow them down!"

"No, *Lord Morgrave*," the man named Simms snapped back. "I'm done with this madness, I'm done with your machinations, and most of all, I'm done with you! This is where it ends," he declared, reaching for the reins of Morgrave's horse. "You have forced me to do your bidding by threatening the life of my family at every turn. But I refuse to be your pawn any longer, my lord." With a fierce glare, the man spat, "Let the lady go. You've burned down her house—what more do you want from her?"

Morgrave's black eyes gleamed with twisted obsession. "You stupid man. Look at her! She's my fire princess—my future. My salvation. She's the woman I've dreamed of having my entire life. The only one worthy of me. The princess of fire—the woman I will take with me into eternity. Fire brought her to me. And I will never let her go." Morgrave jerked Emma by the hair closer to him. She cried in pain as Michael galloped toward them. "And no one will stop me!" the viscount yelled, his voice dripping with malice. In a swift movement, he pulled a pistol from his pocket and fired at Simms, who fell to the ground, clutching his gut.

Michael's heart raced as he charged forward, desperate to reach Emma.

As the clouds shifted once more, a shaft of moonlight illuminated the area, and he watched as Emma pulled a knife from her pocket and plunged it into the soft flesh beneath Morgrave's arm.

"Argh! You bitch!" he roared, fury blazing in his eyes as he slapped her across the face, knocking her to the ground. "I should kill you for that."

Michael saw a haze of red as rage took hold of him. Finally, within a few feet of Morgrave, he leaped from his horse onto the viscount, driving his fist into the man's face and throwing him back.

But Morgrave was stronger than Michael had thought. He quickly ripped the knife from beneath his arm and plunged it into Michael's leg. They both tumbled off the horse.

While Michael felt the stabbing pain in his leg, his fury drove him forward as he kicked Morgrave in the gut, sending the older man reeling backward. Pulling the knife out, he tossed it aside and then leaped onto Morgrave and proceeded to smash his fist into the arsonist's face. "You bastard. You hit Emma. I should kill *you* for that."

"Michael, stop!" Wright shouted from behind.

Michael kept pummeling Morgrave over and over, turning his face into a bloody pulp.

"Enough!" Armstrong said as he and Wright pulled Michael

off the now-unconscious man. "He will be brought to justice for all his crimes, but do not ruin *your* life in the process."

Michael shook them off and stumbled back. Regaining his footing, he spun around and ran to Emma's side. She was lying on her back.

"God, please be alive," he choked out. "Please be alive."

Gently, he placed a finger on the side of her neck and heaved a sigh of relief when he felt the pulse.

"Thank God!" She was alive—but unconscious, and that still worried him.

Carefully, he checked for broken bones and was relieved there were none, but her head was bleeding. He took the monogrammed handkerchief out of his pocket and held it to her head to stem the flow of blood.

Glancing up, he saw that Armstrong and Wright had hauled Morgrave onto his horse and tied his hands and feet to the animal. Meanwhile, they'd assisted the other man, named Simms, back onto his horse.

Bending down, Michael placed a gentle kiss on Emma's lips.

"I love you, Emma," he whispered as he cradled her against his chest.

It was over. *It was finally over.*

CHAPTER TWENTY-ONE

Wilton Hall
Amberley, South Downs
Sussex, England
Several hours later

*P*LEASE WAKE UP, *Emma. Please wake up.*

Michael kept saying the words in his mind over and over like a mantra as he sat by her bedside.

He'd ridden like the devil back to his house, with Emma in his arms, leaving Armstrong and Wright and the other footmen who'd shown up after they heard the gun go off. They could deal with that bastard Morgrave and his servant Simms. He had no idea if Simms would survive or what would happen to him regarding his involvement in Morgrave's crimes, but at this point, he didn't care. All he could think about was Emma.

She'd murmured a few words and then fallen unconscious on the ride back. When he got to the house, he'd rushed up the front steps, kicking open the front door and almost knocking over poor Stanhope, who was just coming to open it.

Michael had barked out orders as he ran up the staircase, for Dr. Bianchi, Celia, Doris, and everyone else to see to Emma's injuries. He could hear Lady Beadle and Aunt Chippie bickering as they came to see what the commotion was about. But that didn't concern him either. Stanhope could play referee between them.

But he had faith in his staff and, yes, in Doris and certainly Celia, who came upstairs moments after he kicked open Emma's bedroom door. They ushered him out while they undressed Emma and called him back inside after she was in bed.

Hastings escorted Dr. Bianchi in a few minutes later. Michael quickly explained her injuries—the rope burns and the injury to her head—and asked that the doctor examine her thoroughly. He'd already taken Celia aside and asked her and Doris to stay. He'd also asked Celia to request that the doctor examine Emma to make sure Morgrave hadn't violated her. Celia assured him that they would do everything to make sure all of Emma's injuries were tended to.

He sighed with relief, and then his knees buckled, and he nearly fell from his leg wound and the resulting blood loss. Luckily, Hastings had grabbed him by the arm and helped him to his own room, where he proceeded to help him undress and wash the grime away, especially on his leg.

Dr. Bianchi bustled in an hour later, just as Hastings was applying pressure to the wound that continued to bleed.

"How is Emma?" Michael asked, feeling his chest constrict at the serious look on Dr. Bianchi's face.

"Calm yourself, my lord," the doctor said as he set his medical bag on the bedside table. "We examined Lady Emma thoroughly, and other than the injury to the back of her head, which required a few stitches, she had only a few minor cuts and bruises in addition to the rope burns on her wrists and ankles. And that is all," he said meaningfully as his eyes met Michael's. "No other injuries of any kind. I left her in the good care of the ladies. She did awaken while I was examining her and was able to answer my questions fully. She is lucid, and she will make a full recovery."

Michael let out a deep breath. "Thank you, doctor."

"But she was very agitated and wanted to know if *you* were all right, my lord."

"What did you tell her?"

"I said you would tell her yourself when you saw her."

Michael rolled his eyes. "I hope you reassured her."

"I did, of course. Now, let us tend to your leg so that you can go to Lady Emma and reassure her yourself, hmm?"

"I might need a few stitches on this damn leg," Michael muttered.

"I think you might need more than that, my lord," Dr. Bianchi said as he examined the wound. "Tell me everything that happened before and after you were stabbed."

Michael told the doctor about the mad ride on horseback to catch up to Morgrave to stop him from kidnapping Emma, and then how he'd leaped onto Morgrave's horse and sent them both toppling to the ground just as Morgrave stabbed him in the leg. They fought, and Morgrave was subdued. He didn't go into further detail about that part—that he had beaten Morgrave to a pulp. But given the good doctor's arched brows, he must have figured it out.

"How is he, doctor?" Wright asked. He and Armstrong had just come up to the room and were standing just inside with their backs to the door. It was as far as Dr. Bianchi and Hastings would allow, both saying they needed a large, uncrowded area around Michael to keep the wounded area clean.

"I think he may be very pleased with my findings. Give me just a minute to check what I'm seeing," Dr. Bianchi said, still probing into the wound. "My lords, I think the stabbing of Lord Wilton's leg, along with the heat of battle, led to something quite extraordinary. If you'll just lie still as can be, I shall show you what I mean momentarily."

"I shall be as still as a log, Bianchi," Michael replied.

"Good, but just in case, we'll have Hastings's help."

With a quick nod, Hastings held down Michael's leg while the doctor proceeded to disinfect the wound. Michael hissed at the sting but, true to his word, kept still as the doctor took a pair of tweezers and began to poke around in the wound. A few moments later he pulled out a small piece of twisted metal and held it up to the candlelight.

"Aha, there we have it."

"Was that from the knife?" Michael asked. Did the tip of the knife break off and lodge itself in his leg?

"No, my lord. This is a piece of shrapnel left over from your old injury. It must have become embedded deep in the bone and then loosened from the stabbing and the fall from the horse. It appears that the knife hit your thigh bone, likely hitting an area impacted by this old wound. Perhaps right alongside it. As I understand it, damage from the previous gunshot wound is the source of your limp and ongoing pain. I've always suspected there was shrapnel still in there, and now, it appears a large piece has been dislodged. It was buried deep in the bone and was probably unable to be detected at the time." He waved his hand in the air in a flourishing movement, as if making the point.

"Lady Bethany Romney thought she had gotten all of it," Armstrong said.

"And she probably did retrieve all she could find. But this larger fragment had embedded itself deep in the bone. The knife's tip struck it and broke it free. Remarkable!" Dr. Bianchi said. "I've no other explanation for what appears to be a true silver lining for this man."

"Well, if you'll excuse me for not being as thrilled about this as all of you are, could you please sew me up so that I can get back to Emma?" Michael asked.

"Of course," the doctor said with a smile.

"So, if I'm following this correctly, if he gets through the healing and any possible fever that comes with it, he could find himself without the pain he's endured," Hastings said. "Is that correct?"

"Yes, that is exactly right," the doctor said, nodding enthusiastically.

"Indeed," Wright said, looking at Michael. "You used to be a pretty good dancer. I might have to brush up on my skills if I'm to continue to outshine him on the dance floor."

Armstrong nearly choked with laughter. "Yes, that might be a good idea."

Michael laughed too. "I don't know if dancing at balls is in my future. But rest assured, I won't be vying for any of the ladies." The only woman he wanted was a few doors down the hall.

As the doctor finished sewing him up, Armstrong and Wright updated Michael on Morgrave and Simms. Morgrave was in bad condition, so they would have Dr. Bianchi patch him up, just enough to transport him under guard to Newgate. Simms's wound wasn't as serious, as the bullet had passed through his side and didn't hit any organs. He told them what had been going on, and Armstrong planned to verify as much as he could and check on Simms's background. If what he told them was true, the man didn't have any prior knowledge of Morgrave's evil deeds and was trying to get out from under the viscount's thumb.

Michael agreed that it would be wrong to turn Simms in to the authorities. They would figure out how they could help him reclaim his life and make up for what he'd done.

An hour later, Michael was at Emma's bedroom door, knocking softly.

Celia opened the door and ushered him in.

"She's resting. She was very upset and wanted to know how you were, until we explained that you were fine and would be in to see her soon. I'll be downstairs if you need me," she said.

"Thank you," Michael said.

"My husband and Lord Wright stopped by ahead of you and then went downstairs to have a hearty meal. I'm sure both he and Wright are being fussed over by Lady Beadle, Aunt Chippie, and Mrs. Peppers," Celia said with a wink as she left the room, closing the door with a soft click.

Michael stood at the foot of Emma's bed for a few moments, taking in the heartwarming scene.

Katie was sound asleep next to Emma with her thumb in her mouth, and at the foot of the bed lay Finn, who had a large bandage wrapped around his torso. Poor fella. Finn was a true hero today. Michael gently rubbed his head, and the dog let out a sigh in his sleep. "Good boy," Michael whispered.

He sat in the chair next to Emma's bed and watched the woman he loved as she slept, her head wrapped in a bandage. She looked so frail. He swallowed a sudden lump in his throat, wishing he could take her in his arms and kiss her. He'd come so close to losing her…

But he would never let that happen again.

He would tell her how he felt.

When she opened her eyes.

"I'll tell you then," he whispered, lifting her hand to his lips and kissing it. "I'll tell you how much I love you, Emma…"

And then he, too, fell asleep.

CHAPTER TWENTY-TWO

S OMETHING WAS MAKING an awful lot of noise.

A whirring sound.

And talking.

"Auntie, it's me, Katie. You must wake up. Finn's worried, too. Except right now, he's sleeping, like you. Finn got hurt, Auntie, but the doctor said he's going to be as good as new. I'll bet he tells you the same thing." Katie crawled up on the bed to kiss her aunt on her closed eyes before sliding back down to the floor. "Just like you always give me, Auntie." The little girl stepped back.

Emma, still feeling very tired, opened her eyes to see her niece standing next to her, and suddenly realized what was making that noise.

Finn! He was sleeping at the foot of her bed, snoring loudly.

She giggled.

"Auntie Emma, we were so worried about you. That bad man took you. Finn tried to save you and got hurt, but the doctor said he's going to be fine. Thank goodness I brought Polly in here to watch over Finn and you," Katie whispered, holding up her doll.

Emma nodded. "Thank you, Polly, for watching over us. And Finn is most definitely a hero." She placed a gentle kiss on Katie's forehead. "And don't worry, I'm here, sweetheart. I'm just a little bruised, but I'll heal quickly. I'm not going anywhere without you, Katie. Don't worry."

"I'm so glad you're back. Lord Michael saved you and brought you home. And he wouldn't leave your side. Look."

Emma turned and was surprised to see Michael seated next to her bed. He, too, was sound asleep.

Tears sprang to her eyes. "Lord Michael is a hero too," she whispered.

"We've got two heroes right here," Katie said with a yawn.

"Let's go back to sleep. We all need to rest," Emma said as her own eyes once more grew heavy. She kissed Katie again and then turned and gazed at Michael and, in a soft voice, said, "I love you, Michael." And then she closed her eyes and fell asleep again.

Sometime later, Emma opened her eyes to see the spaniel and Katie next to her bed, watching her. Finn raised a paw and touched her arm, bringing Emma's gaze to the dog. "Oh! Finn, I'm so glad to see you are here. You are a true hero to me, and I love you, little fella," she said, her gaze moving slowly from Finn to a now-awake Michael as her eyes closed again.

⫸⫷

MICHAEL'S HEART HITCHED. He wished she would say those words to him. Maybe she would one day. "Your aunt will be better soon, angel," Michael said, kissing Katie on her head. "She's strong, but she's been through an awful ordeal and needs her rest now."

"Michael, would it be all right if I leave Polly next to Auntie for a while longer?" Katie asked. "She's very good at making you feel better, but I don't think Auntie Emma has started feeling better yet. And Polly is also good at watching over you."

"That's a really wonderful idea. Polly will be an excellent nurse," Michael agreed, taking the doll and tucking her under one of Emma's arms. "I'll put Polly here, so she can be as close as possible to your auntie."

"Polly watched over Finn when he got hurt. And it made him feel better," Katie said. "But I think she needs to stay longer with Auntie."

Michael looked at Finn, who was lying next to Katie's feet, and could tell that the dog was struggling, but his need to be with the little girl had somewhat overruled his good sense. Michael had heard that spaniels tended to work through pain, even excessive pain. That was how Finn kept going when he'd been in the hull of that ship, starving.

"Katie, did Dr. Bianchi mention anything about Finn getting lots of sleep?" he asked.

"Oh, yes. He told me I should be quiet around him and let him nap. I let him sleep. But now he wants to play," Katie said, giving Michael her sweetest smile.

"Sweetling, I think Finn's side may be hurting him a lot. He has blood on the bandage," he said.

"He does?" Katie asked, walking around to the other side of Finn, where he'd been injured. "Oh, Finn. You're bleeding," she cried out, sounding anguished.

"Perhaps you should take him back to your room and read to him, and let him cuddle up on his bed," Lady Beadle suggested, walking into the room. "But first, I need a hug," she added, pulling Katie close. Then the older woman leaned over and kissed Finn on the head.

"Finn needs another nap, so I'll take him to my room, where his bed is, Lady Beadle," Katie said, leading Finn from the room.

"Precious child," Lady Beadle said. "She's been worried sick about her aunt. I'm so glad you found her." Her tone turned serious. "But you need some rest, too, Michael Robinson. And I won't hear *no* for an answer," she said, patting the pocket where she'd been keeping her ear horn since her arrival. "I don't want to have to tell Lizzy that I failed to take care of her brother while he was on my watch. We just celebrated your birthday. She's going to be upset enough that she couldn't be here to celebrate with you."

Michael laughed. "I will. I promise." Before he left London, Lizzy had sent word that she would be visiting him here, a notice that added more urgency to his need to get the house in decent shape.

Hastings stepped into the room. "My lord, Dr. Bianchi wants to check on Lady Emma again, but he also plans to check on your wound. He needs to change the dressing and do his best to keep it from becoming infected and fevered. We both know how bad that can be."

The man's tone suggested he wasn't taking *no* for an answer either, which amused Michael. But he was in no mood to quibble anyway. He had been watching Emma sleep most of the night, and she was safe. That was all he wanted to focus on for the time being.

"Fine. I'll meet you in my room. Just give me a few more minutes with Emma before I leave."

He heard his valet say, "Stubborn man," as he left the room, and laughed.

Everyone had finally gone, so he moved his chair closer and sat down next to Emma before taking her hand.

"Emma, there's so much I want to say. But I will limit it to three things. First, I will be back as soon as Bianchi is finished checking my wound. Second, you are the most beautiful woman I've ever met—inside and outside. No one in my life could come close to how I see you, my sweet Emma." He leaned down. "And I love you, Emma. Please get well, so I can ask you something very important." He placed a kiss on her lips before standing up to leave. "I hope you heard me. But if you didn't, I plan to say it over and over. I love you."

EMMA OPENED HER eyes, and sunlight was streaming into the room.

Katie was asleep, curled up under her right arm, with her doll in her hands. And Finn was still curled up on the bottom of the bed, snoring away. She thought she remembered them standing next to her, but maybe that had been part of her dreams. She wasn't sure.

"You're awake," Michael whispered in a raspy voice.

A gasp escaped her as she turned to her right and then felt a head rush.

"Careful," he said, moving forward to place a gentle hand on her forehead. "Would you like some water?"

"Yes, please."

He poured her a cup of water from a pitcher on the bedside table and helped her sit up as he held the cup to her lips.

"Better?"

"Yes, thank you."

He set the cup down on the table and then helped ease her back on the pillows.

"How are *you*?" she asked softly.

"I'm better, now that you're awake." He grinned. "And you?"

"I'm better now that you saved me. You're a hero."

"Well, a man has to save one or two damsels in distress if he's going to be called a hero," he said, chuckling.

Emma plucked at the coverlet. "I'm sorry I didn't listen to you about going out of the house without an escort. Are you angry with me?" she asked, her voice trembling with worry. "I was caught up in the excitement of your party and had forgotten part of your present. I had polished the penknife we found in the attic, and I wanted to give that to you along with the salve. I was very foolish."

"You don't have to apologize, Em," he said, leaning forward and taking her hand in his. "It was my duty to protect you, and I failed at that. And for that, I am truly sorry."

A single tear rolled down her face. Michael reached out and brushed it away.

"Well, at least the penknife came in handy," he said.

"Yes, I managed to stab Morgrave."

"And then he used it on me. Stabbed it right in my bad leg. And it was the best stabbing ever."

"What?" she said, as more tears began streaming down her cheeks. "I didn't know he stabbed you. They didn't tell me. They said you were fine—I'm so sorry."

"And I *am* fine," he said. "I didn't tell you that to upset you, darling." He scooted his chair forward, closing the distance between them. "Please...you have nothing to apologize to me about. That was the best gift I've ever received, I think."

His words, unbelievably warm, wrapped around her like a comforting embrace.

"But how? I didn't even have the chance to give it to you," she said, sniffling. "And then that horrible man stabbed you with it."

"I loved the salve and the handkerchiefs. I found several, and they are beautiful." He held one up to show her. "But this particular gift, this penknife...may have led me to no longer needing the salve. Although you worked wonders with it."

"What do you mean?" Emma tried to sit up, but her head began to throb from the exertion, and he helped her lie back down.

"Keep your head on your pillow, darling," Michael said, smoothing the damp hair from her face. "According to Dr. Bianchi, it dislodged a piece of shrapnel that had been undetectable in my bone. He found it while cleaning and stitching the wounds. Bianchi hopes that it will heal, and if it does, I may lose the limp—or at least the chronic pain. Not the scarring, of course. My leg won't be pretty to look at. But hopefully it will heal properly. If not for the lovely present—that very handsome penknife that I will forever treasure—I might never have been given true relief. Luckily, Wright found the thing and returned it to me." He leaned down and kissed her head.

"You're telling me the truth?" she said, astonished.

"I have never lied to you, Emma," he said softly.

"No…you haven't," she agreed. "It's just that it's hard to believe."

"I suppose it was fated, as they say," he said, his lips curved up in a smile. "Pretty soon this house will be abuzz, and you'll have nonstop visitors, and we'll have no privacy." His laughter was warm with affection. "And it's very important that I tell you…That I love you, Emma. I think I fell in love with you on the very first night we met."

"You love me?" she said, in wonder.

"Yes. Is that so hard to believe? Or have I been such a complete grump that you had no idea I'd fallen head over heels in love with you?"

"Well, I sort of had an idea that you liked me enough to keep kissing me. Which I really enjoyed and hopefully will again."

He laughed as he leaned down and kissed her lightly on the mouth. "Oh, we will definitely be kissing again," he said with a growl.

"Good, because I love you too," she said as her eyes blurred with tears.

He kissed her again. "I wanted to tell you how I felt and that I want to spend the rest of my life with you yesterday, after the party was over, but then you went and got yourself kidnapped," he said with a wink.

"I promise, no more getting myself kidnapped." A radiant smile broke out across her face.

"Good, because I would like to make you my countess, that is…if you say yes."

This was everything she had ever dreamed of happening, yet she'd never imagined finding a man she could love as deeply as Michael. "Yes, I will marry you, my lord. As long as you promise to teach me to fish, like you promised, and never get grumpy when I'm trying to do something nice for you."

"All right, you have a deal. But let's kiss on it just to make it official."

"Yes, we must make it official," she said, giggling.

He beamed at her. "I'd love to teach you to fish. And I suppose we should even discuss teaching you and Katie to swim. With the pond so close on this property, I want to ensure we avoid any mishaps."

"I can't believe this is happening," she whispered. "I heard you…earlier."

"When?"

"You told me three things…and I listened to each one. Even though I tried, I couldn't answer you…" Emma said.

"Are you going to marry Lord Wilton, Auntie?" a sleepy Katie said.

"Looks like what we were discussing will have to wait…" Michael whispered teasingly.

"Yes. I'd like to discuss that further," Emma said, then turned to Katie. "I am," she said, kissing her niece on the forehead.

"Oh, goody! It's about time! Isn't it, Finn?"

The spaniel gave a soft woof.

"See, Finn approves. When is the wedding?" Katie asked.

Emma and Michael looked at each other and burst into laughter.

There would be plenty of time to plan a wedding. In the meantime, Emma would insist on more kissing. And she wouldn't have it any other way.

EPILOGUE

Wilton Hall
Amberley, South Downs
Sussex, England
One year later

"DARLING, WE JUST received the sweetest letters from Katie and Evie. Evie and Martin just finished renovating a townhouse in Mayfair," Lady Emma Wilton said from the blue damask settee in the parlor. "Evie says that Katie is doing a wonderful job learning her letters and her numbers with her governess, Jane. And she's loving being Leo's big sister."

"Leo's almost a year old now, isn't he?" Michael asked.

"Yes. Katie helps with his bottle feedings and tells him sto-ries—mostly adventures that she and Finn had while she was here, according to Evie," Emma said, smiling and shifting slightly in her chair, hoping to find the right spot so her back wouldn't hurt. She suddenly realized how miserable Evie must have been when trying to sleep while pregnant. Michael's birthday was tomorrow, and she and Hastings had been planning a small house party for months, hoping to make up for the one last year, which had resulted in her kidnapping.

"Katie's letter was all about how much she missed Finn. It'll be a big surprise when we gift her one of Finn's puppies," she continued. "She will love it. And Martin and Evie will help her train the puppy. They've already approved her having it."

"It'll be nice to see the puppies when they are finally born. Finn is acting like an anxious father—and he struts around here now," Michael said. "Simms said Finn's been very protective of the mother. Not to change the subject, but I'm glad that Simms and his wife and daughter now live on the estate. I understood his not wanting to live in the gamekeeper's cottage. The man's a real talent. The quaint cottage he built near the stables showed masterful carpentry."

"I'm very happy about that," Emma said, "given that Simms was as much a victim of Morgrave's treachery as others were."

"When the puppies are the right age, we'll make a trip to London to bring one to Katie ourselves," he said.

"Yes! I'd enjoy a trip to London. I miss my sister so much. And Katie. I'll be glad to see them for the party."

"I always enjoyed having Katie here. I was never sure how I would react around children, having only been around adults, but a child is fun company," Michael said, exhaling a big breath as he balanced on the ladder, setting the hammer down on the step. "But I think I'll make a jolly good father one day. What do you think, darling?"

Emma smiled a secret smile. "I think you'll be the best father ever."

"Well, maybe not the best." He grinned. "Certainly, in the top three, though."

She giggled as she folded the letter and placed it on the table.

"Darling, are you certain you want these green curtains taken down? We've tried the gold-and-white ones."

"I miss the blue ones. I think they might look better than the gold and white or the green. And besides, blue is your favorite color," Emma said, studying the window. "I think I like those the best," she said with a nod.

"Once I finish hanging these blue curtains, I hope we can both enjoy them for at least a month before you change your mind again," Michael teased, driving a nail into the wall and attaching the drapery rod. "There's only one other thing we need in this room." He hopped down from the ladder, reached behind the settee, and pulled out a brown, wrapped package. "I'd like to hang this over the fireplace, if you agree."

Emma opened it and stared. "This is beautiful! When did you have it painted?"

"I visited Mr. Burns a few months ago and took him up on his offer to paint it. It's an excellent likeness of you and Katie and Finn. I thought you'd enjoy it in your parlor."

"I love it, Lord Wilton!" she said, hugging him around his neck.

"And I love you, Lady Wilton," he said, kissing her.

"You are the best husband in the world."

"Well, *that* I won't argue with." He grinned. "So…when are you planning to tell me?" he asked, leaning in and kissing her softly.

"Tell you what?" she replied, her voice dripping with feigned innocence, a playful smile dancing on her lips. Her heart raced as she turned to face him.

"I know every inch of your beautiful body. And I've watched it change," he said, his gaze shrewd yet tender.

She couldn't help but smile wider, the warmth of his words enveloping her. "I should have known you were too observant," she teased, her cheeks flushing with pride and sudden shyness. "I was hoping to tell you tomorrow after the party as my own special private gift to you. I'm three months pregnant," she added softly.

He whooped as he picked her up and twirled her around the room.

"I take it you're happy?" she said, giggling.

"Honey, you made me the happiest man in the world when you said yes to my marriage proposal, and now you've made me happier, if that's even possible. I knew I couldn't be seeing things," he added. "And I was so hoping it was true."

"Good, because I'm happy too. Sometimes, I have to pinch myself at how happy I am."

"Have you seen all the pinch marks on *my* arms, love? Every day is a wonder, because of you."

"Darling, you're going to be a wonderful father."

"And you are going to be the best mother."

"But now, my surprise gift is ruined."

"Well, you can make it up to me."

"I'm sure you have lots of ideas on that front," she replied, giggling again.

"I can think of a couple of things," he said suggestively. "What about we start with a leg massage?" He winked at her.

"Hmm. Yes. A leg massage you shall have, later, when we've retired for the evening. But I really want to finish a couple of things on my list, darling." If it wasn't for all the guests arriving tomorrow, she would have raced him up to their bedroom. Ever since their marriage, massages had taken on a whole new meaning and become a wonderful treat for both of them. "Michael, I realize I must seem overly focused on making changes, but it's important to get as much done as we can before summer arrives," she said, adjusting the fabric of her dress with care. "I'm not sure I'll have the energy to do much in the heat when I'll be so close to giving birth."

"Emma, darling, I doubt being nine months pregnant will slow you down. Watching you makes me tired," Michael said.

An hour later, she and Michael had gone over everything on her list, making sure that all was ready for their visitors. According to the responses she'd received, everyone would begin arriving for the party in the morning, although both Evie and Michael's sister Lizzy indicated they might arrive tonight. Lizzy and her husband, Baron Edward Sinclair, Lady Beadle, Aunt Chippie, Wright, and the Armstrongs were all planning to attend the house party.

"I'll admit," Michael said, stepping down from the ladder and gazing at the window treatment, "I do like the blue better. These darker curtains cut more of the sun out. I could see myself napping in here on a hot summer day."

She laughed. "Ever the practical one. That wasn't what I wanted to hear. But all right. That's the last change we had to make here in the parlor."

"By the way, I got a missive from Armstrong early this morning," Michael said in a somber tone. "He said the Crown convicted Lord Morgrave of kidnapping a peer, arson, and murder. He will hang at Newgate within the fortnight."

A shiver skittered down Emma's spine. "He is a vile and evil man, and he deserves to pay for his crimes," she said, her voice trembling.

Michael took her in his arms and held her close.

"But what happens to his properties? Or what's left of them? He stole a lot of money, didn't he?" she asked.

"He did, darling. You have a good memory," Michael said. "The families of victims were told to look over the jewelry that was found in his possession, and claim what was theirs, as long as they could provide proof. And of course, the money was divided among all the families, including Evie and Martin."

"That seems more than fair. Michael, would you mind if we change the subject?" she asked. "I'm sorry. But the mere mention of that man still upsets me." And she recalled the day he'd kidnapped her as if it were yesterday, instead of a year ago. Even now, she still had nightmares sometimes. Luckily, Michael was there beside her to hold her when she would wake up in the middle of the night, crying.

"Of course, darling. I'll let Simms know as well," Michael said.

"He's been a great addition as groundskeeper. Finn certainly likes him," Emma said. And Mrs. Simms was a wonderful housekeeper and kept the house running like a well-oiled clock.

"Speaking of Finn, here's the proud daddy-to-be now," Michael said, as Finn sauntered in alongside his partner.

"What beautiful puppies they will make," Emma said. "I can't wait to see them. And I hope each of them behaves just like Finn."

Stanhope knocked on the door and stepped into the parlor. "My lord, Lord and Mrs. Armstrong and Lady Millicent Beadle have arrived."

Michael looked at Emma and then back at Stanhope. "Has Mrs. Simms prepared their rooms?"

Stanhope nodded. "Yes, my lord. The rooms are ready."

"Perfect! Stanhope, could you please show them to their rooms and ask them to join us in the drawing room in two hours for a light repast? Could you ask Mrs. Peppers to prepare something?" Emma said. She hadn't thought the guests would arrive so early today, but she felt content, especially thinking about the good news she had already shared with Michael.

TWO HOURS LATER, Armstrong, Celia, and Lady Beadle joined Michael and Emma in the drawing room. Mrs. Peppers had prepared an informal buffet dinner of finger sandwiches, cheeses, meats, and fruits, as well as a variety of small pastries.

Emma greeted her friends warmly. "I'm so glad to see you again, Lady Beadle and Lady Armstrong. Are your accommodations suitable for your needs?" She hugged them both as they entered the drawing room.

Armstrong shook hands with Michael. "It's good to see you, my friend. Wright will be joining us soon with Aunt Chippie."

"Did I hear right? Chippie will be here?" Lady Beadle asked, gripping her ear horn. "I haven't seen her since last year. Don't tell her I said this, but it will be nice to see her. I rather enjoy sparring with her."

Emma giggled. "I know that's true. We enjoy having both of you."

Laughter filled the Wilton drawing room as carriages continued rolling up the drive and wheels crunched on crushed oyster shells. Each of the guests was directed to freshen up in their room, rest, and join the others in the drawing room, where Mrs. Peppers and Mrs. Simms made sure that the food was plentiful.

"This sounds like the right place, with all that good cheer spilling out," Baron Edward Sinclair—Sin to his friends—said. He and Lady Lizzy Sinclair walked into the drawing room. "I hope you don't mind. We just arrived and were immediately assailed by the delicious scents of Mrs. Pepper's cooking. I recall it from the wedding and couldn't wait to dig in."

"Yes, my husband enjoys a good meal, and I love Mrs. Pepper's lemon tarts. I do hope she made them," Lizzy said, after making the rounds and greeting everyone.

"Oh, she made them," Emma said. "I especially requested them, because I love them too."

"Do I get a hug, sister?" Michael asked, stepping from behind the table to hug Lizzy. "It's been too long since I've seen you, dear girl. I hope you'll consider spending a few extra days."

"We planned to do just that, once your wife suggested it," Sin said. "I'm hoping to have a chance to get to know my new sister-in-law. Simon, Bobby, and little Edward have already settled into the nursery with their governess."

Lady Beadle piped up. "Emma is a real jewel. Michael is a lucky man, in my opinion."

"You're right there, Lady Beadle," Michael agreed.

Once they sat down, Armstrong said, "It appears that Mr. Simms has turned out to be a good employee. I saw him outside as we pulled up."

"Yes. I'm glad we took the time to have a long talk with him last year as he was recovering from his gunshot wound," Michael said.

"And Mrs. Simms is a wonder. Mrs. Pepper adores her as do all the maids," Emma said.

"Indeed!" Armstrong agreed. "Everyone deserves a second chance. Lord Morgrave blackmailed him, saying he'd hurt Simms's family. It took guts to push back. Morgrave was twisted and, in my estimation, crazy."

Emma heard a commotion outside the dining room. It sounded like Katie. "If you can excuse me, I think we have a couple more guests who have arrived," she said. "I'll return as soon as I can."

As she stepped into the hall, she saw Aunt Chippie, Lord Wright, and Evie and her family. Thrilled, Emma practically ran toward them. They had already introduced themselves to Lord Wright and Aunt Chippie.

"I'm so glad to see you all," she said, as she hugged them all and cooed over her infant nephew. "Thank you all for coming."

"Auntie, can I play with Finn?" Katie asked. "I've missed him."

As everyone joined the others in the dining room, they got their food from the buffet and sat down.

Michael gave Emma that crooked smile, and she smiled in return. "Everyone is here. Should we share our news?" she asked him once another round of wine was served.

"You have news? Of course, we'd love to hear it, my dears," Lady Beadle said. "Michael, it's not often that I get news at the same time as Lizzy. She is quite a sensation in London and hears all the juicy gossip before I do."

Emma looked at her husband, who nodded that she should share. Smiling, she looked at the guests—her friends and family. "We are expecting. If I've calculated it correctly, we should be having a baby around Christmas."

Wright stood and immediately proposed a toast, congratulating both Michael and Emma.

"Little girls like pink,
Little boys like blue.
I'll be a great uncle,
Congratulations, you two!"

He held up his drink. "Cheers! I couldn't think of a better pair of parents. And I'm looking forward to being a doting uncle."

The dining room erupted in cheers, good wishes, and laughter.

AS THE EVENING wound down, Emma sought out her husband across the room. Michael stood. "Thank you all for coming. I'm looking forward to celebrating my birthday with friends and family that I love. My lovely wife has managed to give me the best gift this year—sharing with me that I'm going to be a father. She looks tired, so I'm going to take her wife up to bed. But please feel free to stay up as long as you'd like. If you need anything, please let us know." They left the gathering together.

As the two of them opened the door to their room, Michael turned to Emma. "If you are willing, I'd like to flip our routine a little. Instead of you massaging my leg, I'll massage your feet first. And from there...who knows where we will go?" He gave a suggestive wink.

Michael was the perfect husband and partner, as far as Emma was concerned. He always made her feel special, no matter what they did together. "I'd like that, darling. They are tired and sore." She put her hands around his neck, pulling him close and covering his lips with hers, their tongues dancing in a familiar, sensual dance, exploring and tasting. "I'm a lucky woman, Michael," she said.

"And I'm lucky that I found a woman who was willing to heal a broken earl," he said, tracing her jawline with his finger.

His lips covered hers, and the world outside their room faded away.

About the Author

Anna St. Claire is a big believer that *nothing* is impossible if you believe in yourself. She sprinkles her stories with laughter, romance, mystery and lots of possibilities, adhering to the belief that goodness and love will win the day.

Anna is both an avid reader author of American and British historical romance. She and her husband live in Charlotte, North Carolina with their two dogs and often, their two beautiful granddaughters, who live nearby. *Daughter, sister, wife, mother, and Mimi*—all life roles that Anna St. Claire relishes and feels blessed to still enjoy. And she loves her pets – dogs and cats alike, and often inserts them into her books as secondary characters. And she loves chocolate and popcorn, a definite nod to her need for sweet followed by salty…*but not together*—a tasty weakness!

Anna relocated from New York to the Carolinas as a child. Her mother, a retired English and History teacher, always encouraged Anna's interest in writing, after discovering short stories she would write in her spare time.

As a child, she loved mysteries and checked out every *Encyclopedia Brown* story that came into the school library. Before too long, her fascination with history and reading led her to her first historical romance—Margaret Mitchell's *Gone With The Wind*, now a treasured, but weathered book from being read multiple times. The day she discovered Kathleen Woodiwiss,' books, *Shanna* and *Ashes In The Wind*, Anna became hooked. She read every historical romance that came her way and dreams of writing her own historical romances took seed.

Today, her focus is primarily the Regency and Civil War eras, although Anna enjoys almost any period in American and British history. She would love to connect with any of her readers on her website – www.annastclaire.com, through email – annastclaire author@gmail.com, Instagram – annastclaire_author, BookBub – www.bookbub.com/profile/anna-st-claire, Twitter – @1AnnaSt Claire, Facebook – facebook.com/authorannastclaire or on Amazon – amazon.com/Anna-St-Claire/e/B078WMRHHF.

www.ingramcontent.com/pod-product-compliance
Lightning Source LLC
Chambersburg PA
CBHW072128300726
48975CB00003B/969